PIRATES!
In an Adventure with

GIDEON DEFOE was born in 1975 and lives in London. He is also the author of *The Pirates! In an Adventure with Scientists*, *The Pirates! In an Adventure with Moby Dick* and *The Pirates! In an Adventure with Communists*. You could be forgiven for thinking he is a bit of a one-trick pony.

By Gideon Defoe

THE PIRATES! IN AN ADVENTURE WITH SCIENTISTS

THE PIRATES! IN AN ADVENTURE WITH MOBY DICK

THE PIRATES! IN AN ADVENTURE WITH COMMUNISTS

PIRATES!
In an Adventure with

Napoleon

Gideon Defoe

BLOOMSBURY

LONDON · BERLIN · NEW YORK · SYDNEY

First published in Great Britain in 2008 by Weidenfeld & Nicholson
This paperback edition published 2012

Copyright © Gideon Defoe and Richard Murkin 2008
Map copyright © 2008 by Dave Senior

The moral right of the author has been asserted

Bloomsbury Publishing, London, Berlin, New York and Sydney

50 Bedford Square, London WC1B 3DP

A CIP catalogue record for this book is
available from the British Library

ISBN 9781408824986
10 9 8 7 6 5 4 3 2

Typeset by Hewer Text UK Ltd, Edinburgh
Printed in Great Britain by Clays Ltd, St Ives Plc

MIX
Paper from
responsible sources
FSC
www.fsc.org   FSC® C018072

www.bloomsbury.com/gideondefoe

To Evangeline Lilly, Jennifer Garner, Julie Christie, Phoebe Cates, Wendy James out of Transvision Vamp, Alison Clarkson, Molly Ringwald, Beyoncé, Louise Lombard, Miss France 1998, and that elfin one from the first series of *America's Next Top Model*.

Don't start crying about it now, Sophie.
I warned you this was on the cards.

CONTENTS

Module 13: The Late Tudors
The candidates' debate – Concentrate,
Pirate Captain! – A terrible faux pas

Module 14: Oxbow lakes
Getting up early – The duel – Things
look bleak – Oh no!

Module 15: Asteroids, the vermin of the sky
A piece of driftwood – Not so different
after all – Hallucinations

Module 16: Why are bridges?
A sad memorial – Sea monsters? –
A change of heart

Index

THE GREAT ST
A thrilling chase around Her M

WIND BLOWN GRASSLAND

CLUMP of SEAWEED
~flies get in your face~
MISS A TURN.

A PILE of ROTTING WOOD
-Advance TWO spaces-to get away from the smell.

NOT MUCH HERE EITHER

A DEAD GOAT
-Roll again

THE BEACH
You get bits of jellyfish on your shoes,
~MISS A TURN

INSTRUCTIONS

You will need a dice and *Two Dubloons*. Cut out the playing pieces, stick each one to a *Dubloon*. Cut out the *Laurel Wreath* and assemble.
DECIDE who will be NAPOLEON and who will be the PIRATE CAPTAIN. Roll the dice and move the counters around the board, the FIRST one to the finish WINS~They have to say "To the victor the spoils" and wear the wreath on their head for the rest of their lives.

One

ON FIRE AT
A HUNDRED MILES
AN HOUR

'The best thing about the seaside,' said the albino pirate, 'is putting seaweed on your head and pretending you're a lady.'

'That's rubbish!' said the pirate with gout. 'The best thing about the seaside is building sexy but intelligent-looking mermaids out of sand.'

The rest of the pirates, sprawled out on the deck of the pirate boat for their afternoon nap, soon joined in.

'It's the rock pools!'

'It's the saucy postcards!'

'It's the creeping sense of despair!'

Pretty soon the crew were a tangle of earrings[1] and teeth and cutlasses. Buckles rattled, blades swished and bits of pirate went everywhere. But before they could really get going the doors to the downstairs of the pirate boat crashed open, and out strode the Pirate Captain himself. If you were to compare the Pirate Captain to a type of sedimentary rock – which after types of tree,

---

[1] A popular belief amongst sailors of the time was that gold or silver earrings improved eyesight, and protected the wearer from drowning.

3

creatures, and fonts was the next most popular thing for the pirates to compare stuff to – he would undoubtedly be a slab of polished sandstone, or maybe chert. The pirates all took one look at the Captain and stopped their argument dead in its tracks. Fists froze in mid-swing, and mouths hung agape. The Pirate Captain often had this effect on the crew, but usually it was because they held him in such high regard or because they were dazzled by his fantastically glossy and luxuriant beard. Today though, their sudden speechlessness had more to do with the fact that the Pirate Captain was wearing only a tiny bright-red swimming costume which left nothing to the imagination.

'What's all the racket about, you briney swabs?' bellowed the Pirate Captain, his skin glistening in the sunlight with a strangely oily sheen.

'Sorry, Captain,' said the albino pirate. 'We were just discussing what the best thing about the seaside is.'

'The best thing about the seaside?'

'Yes, sir. We couldn't quite decide.'

The pirates waited expectantly for their Captain's response, and tried not to notice the fit of his trunks.

'Honestly,' said the Pirate Captain, after a pregnant[2] pause. 'I have no idea. What a ridiculous thing to be arguing about.'

And with that the Pirate Captain spun on a shiny heel, and strode back through the heavy wooden doors that led to the inside of the boat. There was an awkward silence as the pirate crew all stared at each other, at a bit of a loss. Pirate feet were shuffled. The pirate in green looked like he was about to say something and then stopped himself. Somewhere, a sea-lion barked.

Back downstairs in his office the Pirate Captain stood in front of his full-length mirror, scooped a

2   Famous lady pirates Anne Bonny and Mary Read both escaped the gallows by 'pleading their bellies'. In those days this meant that they were pregnant, not that they were using recent major belly surgery as an excuse to be eight months late delivering a book.

handful of margarine from a little tub and lathered it thoughtfully into his torso. The office was its usual mess of sextants and astrolabes and half-smoked cigars. On one wall there hung a trophy cabinet that showcased the Captain's awards from previous adventures. There was a faded rosette labelled 'Junior Swashbuckler, Obstacle Race – Bronze', and next to that there was a small cup engraved with 'Pirate Captain, Best Nautical Oaths, Runner Up'. And the only other item was a pom-pom with a pair of googly eyes that was attached to a short piece of ribbon revealing it to be an award for 'Second Most Entertaining Anecdote About A Monstrous Manatee'. The Pirate Captain had just started to gaze a bit sadly at the empty space right in the middle of the cabinet when there was a knock at the door, and so he quickly looked back at his mirror and tried to adopt a businesslike air. The Captain's loyal deputy, the pirate with a scarf, poked his head into the cabin.

'Hello, Pirate Captain, could I have a word?' said the pirate with a scarf.

'Of course you can. And whilst you're here, would you mind doing my thighs?' The Captain gestured to the margarine. 'Brings out the musculature,' he added, by way of explanation. 'I can't quite rub it in at the back there.'

The pirate with a scarf dutifully began to rub margarine into his Captain's hairy thighs.

'Now, what's on your mind, number two?'

'Well, sir.' The pirate with a scarf tried to pick his words carefully, because he knew that under all the fearsome tattoos, his Captain had a sensitive core, like a walrus that had swallowed a baby seal. 'It's just that there tends to be a certain . . . *pattern* to the start of our adventures. Some observers might say we were stuck in a rut, but the lads prefer to think of it as "a reassuring tradition". You know, the crew will be having a discussion about some aspect of the piratical life, then it all gets a bit heated, and then you stride out onto the deck, all teeth and curls, with your pleasant open face, and you settle the matter once and for all by making a keen, pithy observation that cuts straight to the point.'

'That does sound like me.'

'Whereas today . . . it was somewhat less exciting than your usual answers. Not

7

necessarily wrong, but not the usual slap-your-forehead blinding revelation stuff.'

'Aarrr. You noticed?' the Captain sighed. 'Sorry about that.'

'Is something bothering you, sir?'

The Pirate Captain paced the length of the office. Little drops of margarine splashed onto the carpet. 'Truth is, number two, I've been feeling a bit preoccupied.'

'Are you still worried about the boat being taken over by genius babies with huge swollen brains?' asked the pirate with a scarf. 'Because Jennifer worked out the odds of that happening and they're vanishingly small.'

'Hmmm. You'd think so, but they're devilishly clever, those babies,' said the Captain, narrowing his eyes. 'Devilishly clever. But no, it's not that.'

He strode back across the cabin and tapped his calendar, which this year was sea monsters.

'Are you getting bored with the sea monster for March? Is that it?' guessed the pirate with the scarf.

The Pirate Captain *had* been getting bored of looking at March's monster, which was

8

something that had the head of a horse and the forelimbs of an eagle. 'You can't blame me; it's ridiculous,' he snorted. 'How could the thing even swim, for a start? Honestly, I don't know where some of these sea-monster artists get their ideas from.'

'Never mind, Captain. April is the kraken. You like the kraken.'

'I do. You know where you are with the kraken. But anyway, no, it's not that either. What's really bothering me is this contest.' The Pirate Captain pointed to 22 March on the calendar, which he had ringed and written 'Pirate of the Year Awards' next to in big letters. 'Obviously I've got the swimsuit round sewn up,' he added, twanging the elastic in his trunks and casting an appreciative gaze at his own glistening reflection in the mirror. 'Not to mention knot-tying, being all things to all men, first-aid, swaggering, and all the boring technical categories. You can't fault me on the practical side of things. But it's the damned question-and-answer session that bothers me. I don't want to look like an idiot in front of the Pirate King and all the other captains. They can say some very cruel things, you know.'

'I don't think you've got anything to worry about, sir,' said the pirate with a scarf encouragingly. 'We all know how hard you've been working.' He waved at the desk, which was covered in a big pile of ring binders, mind maps and plenty of highlighter pens in all the colours: pink, yellow, blue, green and orange.

'That's true,' agreed the Captain. 'In fact I've never done this much preparation for anything. My brain feels like it might pop with all the piratical knowledge that I've crammed into it.'

The Pirate Captain had some interesting theories on brain science, mostly to do with his idea that the brain was more porous when sleeping, so for the past two weeks he'd arranged for the crew to take turns reading pirate theory to him while he was asleep. He also maintained that he had eight lobes to his brain instead of the customary four, which accounted for his remarkable ability to see all sides of any argument.[3]

'And look at the cover I did for my knot-tying notes.' He waved at one of his ring binders, which had a picture on the front of a well-built woman tying a nautical knot in a snake. 'I spent three days drawing that. And all those index cards that the fellow with the glass eye wrote out for me? Hardly any of them ended up as paper planes!'

'And besides,' added the pirate with a scarf as delicately as he could manage. 'If, for any improbable reason you *were* to lose, you'd still be a winner in our eyes.'

'It's nice of you to say so, but you're my crew, so that doesn't really count, does it? It's the same as your mother telling you "you're quite a catch". To be honest I would like, just for once in my career, to know that I had the respect of my peers.'

---

3 Finding out people's opinions on neurophysiology can be a great way of deciding if they're idiots or not. For example, if your boyfriend or girlfriend ever claims that 'we don't even use 90 per cent of our brains!' then you should leave them as soon as possible.

'The lads all think the award is practically in your hands, Captain. You must have noticed how they've been doing the conga an awful lot of late?'

'They *have* been doing more congas than usual,' said the Pirate Captain, rubbing his chin thoughtfully. 'I just put it down to the carnival atmosphere I try to encourage.'

'They're practising, sir. It's a victory conga.'

The Captain stared out of a porthole and his cheeks flushed with emotion. 'If they can believe in me, by crikey, then I can too,' he said, biting his lip. The pirate with a scarf handed him his handkerchief.

'Thanks, number two. I seem to have something in my eye.'

'It's OK to cry, Pirate Captain.'

'No, really, I have. I think it's this damned margarine. Hell's barnacles, that stings.'

Later that day, down in the boat's kitchen, the pirates were all noisily enjoying a feast. The feast was mostly 'mind food' to aid the Captain's mental preparation, so the table was piled high with Vitamin B supplements, steaks cut into different fish shapes, and several cauliflowers, because they look a bit like brains. The Pirate Captain didn't really like cauliflower, so he helped himself to a gigantic portion, smacked his lips and then secretly shovelled it into a napkin and threw it out of a porthole. For pudding they had jelly.

'Now, lads,' said the Captain, once he had licked his bowl clean. 'As you all know, tomorrow is the Pirate King's Pirate of the Year awards.'

An excited buzz ran around the table.

'The Pirate King!' gasped the pirate with a hook for a hand.

'You mean we'll finally get to see him in the flesh?' asked the pirate with long legs. 'Will he eat you if you get a question wrong?'

'Not these days,' said the Pirate Captain reassuringly. 'Apparently the Pirate King feels that eating three-quarters of his pirate captains every year is counterproductive. He's very wise like that. Anyhow, obviously I've pretty much got it in the bag. But I don't want to take all the credit, because behind every dashing Pirate Captain with sparkling eyes there is a crew of capable rogues. Over the past year, thanks to your hard work, we've consistently hit our targets, as you can see from the various graphs I've hung around the room.' The walls were covered in bar charts, pie charts and line graphs. Pirates tended to skive off maths at school, so they didn't really understand the graphs, but they did like the choice of colours, so they cheered anyway.

'Pirate Captain?' asked Jennifer, the former Victorian lady who was now a pirate, indicating one particular graph. 'What's this one about?'

The Pirate Captain looked over to where she was pointing. 'Ah yes. Climbing up rope ladders. That graph shows quite clearly that there has been more climbing up rope ladders on this pirate boat than ever before. I've also plotted it against the number of chin-ups I can do. Now, the only thing standing between me and that sash is the Pirate Theory test. So I thought it best to prepare by having you lot test me with a few questions. Don't go easy on me! Give me your best shots. To help you not go easy on me, you'll find I've written down the questions I want you to ask on the index cards next to your plates. You in the green, why don't you go first.'

The pirate in green stood up and cleared his throat.

'Pirate Captain,' he began, 'it has often been said that one of the most important features of a pirate is to have a stentorian nose, such as yours. What do you think of that?'

The Pirate Captain pushed his hat off his forehead and made a show of mopping his brow. 'Ooh. Bit of a curve ball there. The answer is yes, it is very important. It symbolises resolve in the face of adversity and a belief in one's own destiny. But it's not just a decorative feature. Because over the past twelve months I have put my stentorian nose to good use, with no less than four daring escapes and a series of dramatic encounters with sharks.'

The pirates gave the Captain a polite round of applause.

'I think that's the right answer, Captain,' said the pirate in green.

'OK,' said the Pirate Captain, 'you next, over there, with the hook for a hand. Have you got a question for me?'

The pirate with a hook for a hand stood up clutching his index card. He was slightly nervous because his experience of public speaking was limited to shouting at seagulls. 'The title of Pirate of the Year is not just an accolade that recognises your superior pirating and extreme good looks, Pirate Captain. It also comes with great responsibility. As a role model to young pirates the world over, what would you do?'

'That's an excellent point and one that I feel has often been overlooked by previous Pirates of the Year, not that I want to name any names, though Jericho Blake, he's one. Gunpowder Gillespie, that's another. Needless to say, I would mainly concentrate on my community work, and certainly not just use the title to take advantage of adoring teenage female pirate fans.'

The pirates roared, apart from the pirate with asthma who wheezed enthusiastically until the

Pirate Captain motioned for calm. 'Thanks, lads. Now you, the pirate in red.'

The pirate in red stayed sitting in his chair. And he didn't even look at the card the Captain had given him.

'If you were to splice the mainsail,' he said, 'what would it actually involve? And how would it be accomplished?' He sat back and folded his arms in a surly way.

The Captain looked annoyed, and tapped his gold teeth for a moment. Then he feigned a large ostentatious yawn and pretended to suddenly notice his pocket watch. 'Goodness me, is that the time? Well, bit tired now, no point over-taxing the lobes. Who's for more jelly?'

'The Pirate Captain's a living legend!' said the pirate who liked kittens and sunsets.

Jennifer leaped to her feet and kissed the Pirate Captain on the cheek. 'Oh, Pirate Captain, you're going to knock them dead!'

'Arrr,' roared the Pirate Captain, rather than blush. 'That's right, my lovelies. I want you to set sail for victory. Victory and pudding!'

Two

BY SLEDGE AND DOG
OVER THE POLAR SEA

Everybody was glad that the Pirate King had chosen to hold this year's award ceremony on Skull Island. There had been a lot of talk about escalating overheads and suggestions that it might get moved to Stoke, but thankfully the powers that be had seen the benefits of parrots and women in coconut bikinis over the conference facilities and excellent road links of Staffordshire's largest city. Pirates from across the globe thronged the picturesque tropical bay, and important piratical gossip – like whether Scarlet Morgan had cellulite and if it was true that Howling Jenkins had been getting out of boats without wearing any underwear – buzzed about the place. The pirate crews made a beeline for the special fair that the Pirate King had laid on to keep them out of trouble. It had a stall where they could throw sharp rocks at a man dressed as an admiral to win cuddly toys, a shop where you could get your face painted as a nautical creature, and a waltzer where the cars were shaped like giant barnacles. There was also an enclosure with some barnyard animals that you could actually stroke.[4]

Whilst his crew had fun, the Pirate Captain stiffened his resolve with a shot of grog mixed with gunpowder and went to mingle with his peers. He didn't really look forward to mingling. It wasn't because he didn't like the other pirate captains, it was more that he knew he'd met most of them before, and yet he could never seem to remember their names or anything about them. And he found they had an annoying tendency to talk about themselves and their adventures, which he considered rude, particularly when his own adventures were much more interesting. But it was important to observe the social niceties, so he strode up the blood-red carpet into the VIP Captains Only marquee as boldly as he could. He had barely got through

---

4 There were several pirate havens. According to *A General History of the Pyrates* by Captain Johnson, who may or may not have been Daniel Defoe writing nonsense, the most successful was 'Libertalia' on Madagascar, an anarchist utopia where the pirates even made up their own language.

the door when a pirate with large eyebrows stepped up and clapped him on the back.

'Pirate Captain! It's great to see you again! You're looking fantastic,' said the pirate. He did that handshake where you clasp the other person's arm to convey genuine warmth.

'Hello there,' said the Pirate Captain, trying to place the familiar face. 'It's great to see you too.' He took a long sip of grog to give himself time to think. After about ten minutes, he felt he should probably stop sipping and say something. 'Peg Leg Hastings!' he chanced. 'Peg Leg! How are you? Had any good adventures lately? Miss your leg? How's the stump?'

The other pirate's big eyebrows drooped as the Captain noticed his two, perfectly intact legs.

'It grew back? Wow! That's quite something. I didn't think they could do that.'

'I'm not Peg Leg Hastings, Pirate Captain.'

'Of course you are,' said the Captain, adopting his usual policy of ploughing on regardless, no matter how high the facts were stacked against him. 'I'd know you any day of the week. We go way back to Pirate Academy.'

'Peg Leg Hastings was a woman.'

'A woman. Really?'

'And she was eaten by cannibals two years ago. You were at her funeral.'[5]

'Fancy that.'

'You read the eulogy.'

'Did I? Was it moving?'

'Quite moving. Though you spent more time giving advice on getting stains out of cravats than talking about her life.'

'Typical me!' said the Pirate Captain, trying to make the conversation breezy again. 'Well then, if you're not Peg Leg Hastings that would make you . . . oh my Lord! Your hat is on fire!'

The Pirate Captain ducked behind a fearsome-looking crowd of Chinese pirates and grabbed a sausage on a stick from a passing waitress. He decided that a good tactic to avoid further embarrassing conversation would be to stand in the corner and pretend to be too busy admiring his sausage on a stick to talk to anyone. He

---

5   A fate that also befell the French buccaneer François L'Olonnais, eaten along with about 700 of his men by the Darien Indians of San Pedro.

was admiring it so hard he barely noticed that an eager-looking young pirate with a side parting had sidled up right in front of him. The Captain sighed.

'Hello,' said the pirate. 'I don't believe we've met?'

The Pirate Captain brightened immediately. 'Haven't we? How fantastic.' He extended a hand. 'I'm the Pirate Captain.'

By way of reply, the pirate with a side parting smiled an oily smile and thrust a little white rectangle towards him. The Captain flinched and drew back in fright, because in piratical circles this sort of thing usually came with a black spot that meant you were marked for a bloody death.

'Steady on,' said the Pirate Captain.

'It's a business card,' explained the pirate.

'Ah. I see.' The Pirate Captain squinted down at the card. It read:

ALAN HINTON, BA (Hons)

– Pirate –

'What a clever idea. I tend to rely on just saying who I am. You know, with my mouth.' The Pirate Captain pointed at his mouth just in case Alan Hinton was a bit simple.

'Mouths are yesterday's mode of communication, Pirate Captain,' said Alan Hinton BA, Hons. 'In the fast-paced, efficient world of modern piracy there's no room for time-consuming introductions.'

'Isn't there? Well, there you go.' The Pirate Captain looked again at the little card. 'So. *Alan Hinton*. Not a very piratical-sounding name. Not much use for frightening the lubbers. What you need is an exciting nickname based on a characteristic you feel really sums up who you are. That tends to be how it works. For instance, if you're particularly bloodthirsty you could have "Bloodthirsty Alan". Or "One-Eyed Alan" if you only had the one eye. Or, I don't know, do you get hungry a lot? "Hungry Alan". No forget that, that one's rubbish. But you get the gist?'

'As you can see,' said Alan Hinton BA, Hons, 'rather than a nickname I have a first-class honours degree in naval studies and business management from Oxford University.'

26

'Aaarrr, well, that's all fine and good,' nodded the Pirate Captain. 'But my degree is from the university of life. Of course, it turns out there is no such place as the university of life, and the entire thousand-doubloon, nine-month correspondence course was just a scam run by Black Bellamy. Still, a certificate is a certificate, that's what my Aunt Joan always used to say. Have you met my Aunt Joan?'

'I'm afraid not, Pirate Captain, I don't have much room in my schedule for meeting people's aunts.'

'Oh, you should meet her. Fascinating woman. Another thing she used to say was "book smarts are no match for a nice hat and a sunny outlook", advice that's helped me on all my adventures.'

Alan Hinton BA, Hons sipped his mineral water. 'Yes. I've read about your "adventures", Pirate Captain.'

'You have?' the Captain grinned. 'It's always nice to meet a fan.'

'As a matter of fact I wrote an essay on you for my piratical history paper at Pirate Academy. I really feel that there's so much the future can learn from the ancient past.'

The Pirate Captain was pretty sure that when Alan Hinton BA, Hons said 'future' he was referring to sharp side partings, and when he said 'ancient past' he was referring to luxuriantly bearded rogues, but he managed to bite his tongue.

'So, Alan. Have you got your speech worked out? Mine is on the theme of "the best summer I ever had". It's about when I worked as a fruit-picker in Kent. There was a rosy-cheeked peasant girl called Naomi. We used to chase each other through wheat fields and sleep under the stars. If I was lucky I'd get tops. Happy days. The best thing is, it took me less time to write than it will to say.'

'The title of mine is "Trajectories: taking piracy into the nineteenth century – a bold new age where fiscal responsibility and embracing new technology are more important than roaring and running people through."'

'Goodness me,' said the Captain. 'I don't think I've ever had an adventure with fiscal responsibility.'

In the Skull Island Anne Bonny Memorial Auditorium the rest of the pirates, laden down with goody bags, bustled about looking for their seats. Jennifer was pleased to find she was sitting at a table with the pirate in green, the pirate with a scarf and the pirate with long legs, because they were the pirates who tended to have the most personality. The pirate in red was also there, which she didn't mind, as long as he kept the sarcastic tone out of his voice. They all gazed about the auditorium with mounting excitement. The pirate in green almost began to hyperventilate as the curtain went up to reveal a stage tastefully dressed in mountains of gold lamé and strings of pearls that were as big as tennis balls, and several dancers dressed as giant clams. In the middle of it all sat a colossal empty throne with a drinks holder in one arm and an ashtray on the other. You could cut the atmosphere with a knife, and there was a rustle of cutlasses as a few of the more literal-minded pirates tried to do just that.

'What do you suppose the Pirate King looks like?' whispered Jennifer.

'I heard that his hands are big enough to crush the Royal Navy flagship in one crush!' said the pirate with long legs. 'And that he can kill a man just by looking at him. And that he's immortal.'

'I heard he's got *three* beards,' said the pirate in green.

'I heard,' said the albino pirate, 'that his voice is so booming it has a special effect on ladies. Something to do with the shape of their pelvises.'

'Sshh!' said the pirate in red with a wave of his hand. 'Here he comes!'

A frail old man wearing a slightly tatty crown emerged from one side of the stage and hobbled towards the throne. He tottered into it before coughing consumptively for a few minutes.

'Fellow pirates,' he eventually croaked in a hoarse whisper. 'It gives me great pleasure to welcome you to my Pirate of the Year awards.'

'He's not *quite* what you'd led me to expect,' whispered Jennifer to the pirate in green.

'We've learned another of those valuable life-lessons here, I assume,' said the pirate in green, looking distraught. 'I'm just not quite sure what it is yet.'

But before the frail old man on the stage could get any further, an enormous explosion went off somewhere near the back of the room, accompanied by the blast of at least fifty trumpets and a hundred gongs. The audience twisted round in their seats to see what was going on. Standing there, wreathed in sea mist, was a figure so awe-inspiring that no description written down in a book could ever do him justice.

'WHO THE BLAZES IS THAT?' roared the figure in a voice that sounded like a whole fleet of ships firing their cannons at a massive sheet of metal. 'GET OFF MY THRONE!' He winked at the audience, who all cheered as he bounded through the auditorium and onto the stage in two huge strides, pausing only to burst a hot water bottle by blowing into it and rip a telephone directory in half. The fake Pirate King quivered in mock terror, but then stopped quivering as he was swept up in one stately hand and thrown bodily into the orchestra pit. Everybody cheered again. The real Pirate King flashed the audience a grin that contained at least as much gold as the Crown Jewels of Britain and Spain put together.

'HELLO, PIRATES,' said the Pirate King.

'Hello, Pirate King,' the pirates yelled back.

'Now *that*'s making an entrance,' whispered Jennifer approvingly.

The Pirate King lit a cigar, leaned back in his throne and blew a smoke ring the size of a life-buoy. 'BY CRIKEY YOU'RE A FINE BUNCH,' he boomed. 'A FINE, FINE, FINE BUNCH OF ROGUES, SCALLYWAGS AND NE'ER-DO-WELLS. IT MAKES ME PROUD TO BE YOUR KING.' He threw back his head and laughed so hard that dust and bits of plaster cascaded from the ceiling.

'ANY LUBBERS IN?'

'No!' chorused the pirates.

'OF COURSE NOT. WHY, IF A LUBBER WAS TO SET FOOT IN THIS HALL, HE'D PROBABLY DROP DEAD ON THE SPOT FROM THE SHEER CONCENTRATION OF GOOD, HONEST BRINE IN THE AIR. BUT WE'RE NOT HERE TO TALK ABOUT

LUBBERS. WE'RE HERE TO GIVE OUT THE PIRATE OF THE YEAR AWARD TO THE BEST PIRATE.'

The Pirate King paused for a moment to pull a great white shark from behind his throne and punch it in half with a fist. A fair amount of shark guts went over the tables at the front, but none of the audience minded at all.

'IT'S BEEN A GREAT YEAR FOR PIRAT-ING,' said the Pirate King, striking a serious tone. 'AND THE YEAR AHEAD IS LOOKING EVEN MORE EXCITING. IN THE COMING MONTHS WE'LL BE LAUNCHING A DRIVE TO ELIMINATE THE WORRYING LEVELS OF OBESITY AMONGST THE PIRATE POPULA-TION. I ALSO HAVE PLANS TO REDUCE HEALTH AND SAFETY HAZARDS ON PIRATE BOATS, SO I'LL BE LOOKING FOR A PIRATE OF THE YEAR WHO CAN HELP ME MAKE THE WORLD OF PIRATING BETTER THAN EVER. THIS AWARD ISN'T JUST ABOUT THE ENDLESS FEASTS AT MY TABLE OR THE FEMALE COMPANIONSHIP OR THE SASH OR THE LIFETIME SUPPLY OF

33

TOOTHBRUSHES. IT'S A POSITION OF REAL RESPONSIBILITY WITH STUFF TO SIGN AND PERSONAL APPEARANCES AT ALL THE TOP EVENTS. SO WITH THAT IN MIND, LET'S HEAR FROM THE FIRST NOMINEE!'

The audience clapped again, and the Pirate Captain sauntered on from the other side of the stage. He straightened his beard and gave his crew a cheery thumbs-up.

'Ooh, here he comes, fingers crossed,' said Jennifer.

The pirate with a scarf couldn't bear to watch, so he covered his face with a napkin.

'SO. PIRATE CAPTAIN. ARE YOU READY?' asked the Pirate King.

'Ready as I'll ever be,' said the Pirate Captain.

'PIRATE CAPTAIN, YOUR QUESTION IS THIS. IF YOU WERE TO SPLICE THE MAIN-SAIL, WHAT WOULD IT ACTUALLY INVOLVE? AND HOW WOULD IT BE ACCOMPLISHED?'

Three

NO SURRENDER –
THE END OF HILL
SQUADRON

The Pirate Captain tried to stare disconsolately into the bottom of his drink, but he kept on poking himself in the eye with the little cocktail umbrella. Drowning his sorrows in the Skull Island paradise-themed lounge bar was proving to be annoyingly difficult. When you're upset, the Captain decided, it was best to have surroundings that matched your mood. To this end he would have preferred a plaintive solo saxophone to be playing in the corner of the bar instead of a five-piece tropical band complete with maracas. And similarly, gazing miserably out of a window would be much more effective if it was streaked with rain, rather than providing a clear view of a high-spirited pool party.

'I've brought you another Exciting Beach Fun, Pirate Captain,' said the pirate with a scarf, handing him a huge bright-red cocktail adorned with a plastic monkey on a stick and with what looked like half a bowl of fruit balanced around the rim. 'Though the fifty doubloons that the Pirate King put behind the bar has just run out, so if you want to go on drowning your sorrows we'll have to start paying.'

The Pirate Captain did one of his bleakest looks by way of reply.

'Cheer up, sir,' the pirate with a scarf added encouragingly. 'You'll bounce back. And there's always next year. Twelfth time's the charm.'

'No,' said the Captain firmly. 'That's it. I can't possibly work any harder than I did this time. I've learnt an important and bitter lesson.' He pointed at an empty space on the bar where his award would have been if he'd won. 'That's what hard work gets you: nothing. Never put any effort into anything, number two. Because it will turn to ashes in your mouth. From now on, the old indefatigable, roll-up-my-sleeves, get-my-hands-dirty, work-ethic Pirate Captain is a thing of the past.'

The pirate with a scarf knew better than to challenge this slightly imaginative description of the Pirate Captain's previous attitude to hard work. He sat down on a bar stool and cast a surreptitious look at the Captain's mood ring. Several years' experience had taught the pirate with a scarf that the Captain's moods rarely lasted more than twenty minutes, less if a distraction came along, like an interesting noise or a cup of tea. This unpredictability could make life in the confined space of the pirate boat quite tricky, and the pirate with a scarf had bought his Captain the ring so that there would be no confusion as to how he was feeling at any given time. Right now the ring was jet black, which either meant 'tense, nervous, harassed' or that all the mood juice had leaked out.

'They didn't even do a swimsuit round,' added the Pirate Captain plaintively.

'To be fair, Captain, they've never done a swimsuit round. That was more hopeful speculation on your part. But if they had done one, you'd have walked it.'

The crew shuffled up to the table, doing a slow conga of disappointment, and singing 'Da na-na na na na-na' in a minor key. The Pirate Captain gave them a weary wave.

'I know you're trying your best, but it's not helping. I think it's pretty much impossible to cheer me up.' The Captain hefted another heavy sigh and snapped his little plastic monkey in two. 'It's like I have a big black dog lying on my heart. And what's worse, it's getting slobber on my aorta and it keeps jumping up and down on my right lung.'

'That's a very poetic analogy, Captain,' said the pirate with a scarf.

'Thank you. Now, if you don't mind I'm going to wail "why?" quietly to myself for a while.'

The Pirate Captain had got to his third 'Why?' when a huge hand smacked his shoulder so hard that there was an audible crack. He looked up to see a burly pirate built like a Welsh mountain range grinning down at him.

'Hello, Pirate Captain,' said the pirate. 'Bad luck with the awards. I imagine you're pretty cut up. But if it's any consolation you're still the best pirate I know, and I know at least four pirates.'

'Thanks, Scurvy Jake,' said the Pirate Captain, wiping Exciting Beach Fun off his coat. Scurvy Jake was an old friend who had retired from pirating because his gigantic sausage fingers made him clumsy. Since then he'd had a series of jobs that had worked out a bit better for him, providing they didn't involve holding easily crushed things like eggs or baby rabbits.

'All the best people aren't appreciated in their lifetimes,' Scurvy Jake continued. 'Look at Baby Jesus – nobody took him seriously. They thought he was a tramp!'

'Oh, let's not talk about me, Jake. I don't think I can face it,' said the Pirate Captain. 'What have you been up to lately? Still working as a grill chef?'

'No, I gave that up. Don't get me wrong, I loved the grilling. I could grill all day. But I hated going home smelling of burnt fat.'

'I can imagine,' said the Pirate Captain, although he couldn't really imagine why that would be a problem because as far as he was concerned, most of the best smells involved meat grease.

'It stays in your hair, you see.' Scurvy Jake was very particular about his hair, which he wore in a permanent wave that he had set every few weeks. 'So I've got a new job now. It's a real money-spinner.'

Scurvy Jake leaned closer to the Pirate Captain's ear and whispered loudly, 'I sell baby clothes door-to-door.'

The Pirate Captain didn't know what to say to that, so he just said 'baby clothes' and raised his eyebrows.

'That's right. The great thing is . . .' Scurvy Jake beckoned the Pirate Captain closer and whispered even louder, 'babies grow so quickly that they need a new set of clothes every few weeks. It's practically a licence to print doubloons!' He paused for a moment to drain his cocktail in one gulp. 'Have a guess how long it takes a baby to outgrow a brand new set of woollen bootees.'

'A month?' said the Pirate Captain.

'Two weeks!' said Scurvy Jake happily. 'Babies are a gold mine!'[6]

'Good for you,' said the Captain, glad his old friend was doing so well. He almost began to cheer up despite himself, but suddenly there was an excited hubbub, and a pack of young pirates with neat clothes and good teeth walked into the lounge bar carrying a trophy-laden Alan

---

6   The biggest baby ever born in Britain weighed 15lb 2oz. But in 1879 an Ohio woman is recorded as giving birth to a 24lb baby. That's 0.0109 double-decker buses!

Hinton BA, Hons on their shoulders. They were all wearing matching pirate blazers and looked extremely pleased with themselves. Alan Hinton BA, Hons waved a glass of Pimms in the Captain's direction and then went back to discussing quarterly yields with the earnest pirate holding his leg. The Captain slumped again.

'Take a look at that,' he said. 'That's the future of pirating right there, all haircuts, spreadsheets and retractable pencils.'

'Aarrr . . .' said Scurvy Jake, who still did pirate noises despite having retired. 'Pirating's a young man's game. Like Twister or spin the bottle.'

'Exactly,' nodded the Captain. 'With my care-free attitude and frank disinterest in ironed clothes, I'm nothing more than a dinosaur.'

Several pirate crew nearby jumped out of their seats and dropped their cocktails in fright.

'Not an *actual* dinosaur,' said the Pirate Captain, rolling his eyes. The pirates breathed a sigh of relief and sat back down again. 'But my point stands – maybe pirating isn't really suited to me any more. Perhaps I should turn my hand to something new. I need to evolve from being a dinosaur into ... what came after dinosaurs? Chickens? Or was it mice? One of those.'

Before long, the pirates were all having a heated argument about evolution, with one side coming down on the side of chickens and the other mice. A breakaway faction proposed tardigrades, but it was suggested that they were simply showing off their knowledge of creatures. Just as chickens were getting the upper hand, the debate was interrupted by an overpowering smell of seaweed, and then Jennifer appeared through the crowd pulling a familiar fearsome figure with her. 'Pirate Captain!' she exclaimed. 'Look who I found, it's Black Bellamy! Your old friend!'

Black Bellamy beamed, in as much as you can beam when your beard goes all the way up to your eyeballs of darkest pitch and you carry a knife between your teeth.

The Pirate Captain swore under his breath. 'He's not my friend, Jennifer. He's my eternal nemesis, whom I have sworn to defeat or die trying. Hello, Black Bellamy.'

'Hello, Pirate Captain,' said Black Bellamy. 'Bad luck about the awards.'

'Listen, BB, that was a pretty low stunt you pulled with the fake whale business on our adventure before last. I haven't forgotten that.' The Pirate Captain frowned. 'So I'm not talking to you. In fact, don't even look at me.' He pointedly swivelled his chair around to face the other way.

'Can I look at Jennifer instead?' asked Black Bellamy. 'She's as lovely as ever, radiant like the moon on a clear night.'

'That's enough of your sexy metaphors,' said the Pirate Captain.

'Similes, Pirate Captain. Sexy similes.'

'All right, you *can* look at me,' huffed the Captain, turning back round again. 'But I'd rather you didn't. And I'm not really in the mood for your tricks right now. I suppose you're here to con me into buying something that explodes and/or turns out to be full of snakes?'

Black Bellamy looked hurt. 'Pirate Captain! It's so very painful to hear you talk like that. All I wanted to know,' he paused and fought back a

45

grin, 'is what kind of pirating you have planned next and whether it involves splicing the main-sail at all?'

The Captain glowered. 'Actually, I don't have any kind of pirating planned next.' He leaned back in his chair and pulled the most resolute face he could do. 'Because from this day forth, *I am no longer a pirate!*'

He waited for the reaction. A couple of the pirates made gasping sounds, but there was something unconvincing about them. The Captain wondered if he should perhaps make a dramatic gesture to go with his dramatic state-ment, like stamping on his pirate hat and flinging it into the sea. But it was an expensive hat so he just mimed it instead.

'I really, really mean it,' said the Pirate Captain, a hint of exasperation creeping into his voice.

'Don't be daft,' said Jennifer. 'Pirating is bril-liant fun. And besides, what would you do instead?'

Black Bellamy seemed bemused. 'Yes, Pirate Captain, what's it going to be this time?'

The Pirate Captain puffed out his hairy cheeks. He hadn't really thought that far ahead. He looked about the cocktail lounge. Failing to find inspiration there he looked at his crew. One of them was wearing a fashionable yellow and black striped top.

'Bees!' exclaimed the Pirate Captain, surprising himself a little. 'I will raise bees.'

'Really?' said Black Bellamy and Jennifer in unison.

'Oh yes. You're probably thinking that I just said "bees" because I happened to look at that pirate in the stripy top and it was simply the first thing that popped into my head, but actually I've been interested in bees all my life. Fact is, I've spent many a pleasant afternoon dreaming about the simple life of a bee-keeper. Tending to them one by one, washing their little bee faces, drawing them pictures of hexagons. Later, perhaps, singing them to sleep under the stars with a tender rustic ballad of times gone by.'

'But, Pirate Captain, you *love* being a pirate,' said Jennifer. 'You're always pointing out the myriad lifestyle benefits. Getting to travel the

47

world, catch exotic diseases and learn about bloody murder and all that stuff.'

'That's because I was looking at piracy through rose-tinted spectacles,' the Captain replied. 'In fact, there's very little job security. The hours are terrible. And those barnacles get everywhere. I found one in my belly button the other day.'

The crew didn't look convinced. The Captain reflected that if they were half as good at pirating as they were at not looking convinced he would be a very rich man, probably with a solid-gold pirate boat. He tried another tack.

'Also, lads, in today's world, given the industrial revolution and all, you have to start thinking ecologically. Remember that adventure we had with those Aztecs? Where, when they wouldn't give us that big diamond skull, we burnt their entire jungle to the ground? Our carbon footprint must be *gigantic*. Not like bee-keeping. Once we're up and running we'll be entirely self-sufficient. That's the great thing about bees. We'll get a constant supply of nutritious honey. We can use their little bee pelts to make warm clothes. And they're a ready source of beef.'

'Beef?' said Jennifer.

'Beef. Beef from the bees. Hence the name.[7]

The pirate crew fell silent for a moment, because it was difficult to argue with environmental matters.

'It sounds like a fine plan, Captain,' said Black Bellamy. 'But you'll be needing some land.'

The Pirate Captain shrugged. 'I was thinking I could just grow them on my boat. Use the cannons as beehives, something like that.'

'Can't keep bees on a boat,' reasoned Black Bellamy. 'There are no flowers at sea.'

The pirates nodded and thought to themselves how the phrase 'there are no flowers at sea' sounded very poignant, and would make a nice tattoo or maybe a good lyric for a sad shanty.

---

7 Another use for bees, as developed by the US Military, is to get them to sniff out bombs. By applying Pavlovian conditioning techniques the bees have been trained to stick their tongues out whenever they smell explosives.

'But by sheer good fortune I think I might have just the thing,' said Bellamy, his eyes lighting up. 'Don't go anywhere, Pirate Captain, I'll be back in a tick.'

Black Bellamy hurried off across the bar to another table where his crew were playing an old pirate drinking game that involved making up names for the Royal Navy, and returned a moment later waving a couple of pieces of paper.

'I know that in the past I've not always been strictly above board with you, Pirate Captain,' said Black Bellamy, looking serious. 'But if you're really giving up pirating then I'd like us to part on good terms. And to show bygones are bygones, I'm going to help you in your new life, because it just so happens that I recently acquired some prime real estate. It's a beautiful tropical island in the Atlantic called St Helena. These are the title deeds.'

Bellamy handed the papers to the Pirate Captain, who looked at them suspiciously.

'Wait a minute, BB. If I know one thing about oceans it's that the Pacific is the nice warm one and the Atlantic is the rubbish cold one.'

Black Bellamy smiled. 'Oh, Pirate Captain, I can see you're as sharp as ever. But you see, there's a trade wind which keeps the whole island at the delightful ambient temperature of . . . what's your favourite temperature?'

'I'm not sure. Thirty-two degrees?'

'Yes, that's it – thirty-two degrees. Perfect bee-keeping weather. Famed for its bees, St Helena is. I hear they grow to the size of dachshunds.[8] I had been hoping to hold onto it for myself, as a relaxing winter holiday home. But I see now that you'll make much better use of the place than me. So I want you to take these entirely bona-fide deeds, Pirate Captain, for nothing more than a nominal friends-only bargain price.'

The Pirate Captain looked again at the papers which Black Bellamy had produced.

---

8 The largest bee in the world, the *Megachile pluto*, is actually 1.5 inches long – that's 0.00416 double-decker buses, or about the length of one giant baby's ears.

Welcome To Sunny St. Helena

'It does look quite nice,' said the Captain thoughtfully. 'And I suppose I *should* give you a chance to make up for your past behaviour. How much are you after, you rogue?'

'Oh, again with the hurtful names. But I won't hold it against you, Captain. So why don't we just say ...' Black Bellamy paused and stroked his beard for a moment. 'A hundred doubloons. After all, you won't really be needing treasure now you're a bee-keeper.'

'That's true,' said the Captain. 'This island. Any inhabitants?'

'Just a full complement of indigenous ladies.'

'Winsome?'

'Very.'

The Pirate Captain mulled things over for a moment. He tried to picture a pie chart in his mind of 'good reasons to stay in pirating' and 'good reasons to go and live on a lush tropical island'. And to his surprise the pie chart didn't even have a missing piece of pie, it was just a big circle, full of relaxing evenings, bucolic bees and native ladies.

He drew himself up to his full height and shook Black Bellamy's hand manfully. 'All right, BB, you've got yourself a deal.'

'You won't regret this, Pirate Captain,' said Bellamy, turning round to give his crew, who all seemed to be suddenly overcome by a fit of giggles, a thumbs-up. 'I think it's the start of a brilliant new career.'[9]

'Of course,' added the Pirate Captain, 'you can't really go on being my nemesis now that I'm a bee-keeper. Unless you fancy giving up pirating too? You could raise wasps.'

---

9   Don't worry if you haven't found your ideal career yet. Lots of famous people were late starters. Buster Merryfield from *Only Fools and Horses* didn't take up acting until he was in his sixties.

Four

UNDER BRAZIL
BY SUBMARINE

Jennifer watched the seagulls circle lazily around the mast of the pirate boat, flicked a barnacle off her cutlass and frowned. She'd expected the other pirates to be distraught at the prospect of becoming a bee-keeping crew. But if anything they were more relaxed than ever. The pirate with gout and the pirate in green were having a competition to see who could look most louche. The pirate with asthma was telling the pirate with a nut allergy about the different kinds of gravy boat you could get nowadays. The albino pirate was trying to train a whelk to do tricks. Even the pirate with a scarf didn't seem particularly bothered. It was, Jennifer decided, obviously up to her to take action.

'Come on, you lot!' she exclaimed, kicking a cannon with her steel-tipped pirate boot to get the crew's attention. 'We can't just muck about when our entire way of life is under threat thanks to the whims of that ... that *man*. It's time to stand up and be counted and fight like proper pirates for everything we believe in!'

A few of the pirates clapped because they felt that was what was expected, but none of them showed any signs of action.

'Listen, do you know what I'd be doing if I was still a Victorian lady instead of a pirate?' Jennifer persisted.

The pirates didn't have a clue, but the pirate with long legs tried a guess. 'Having a shower?'

'No,' said Jennifer, 'I'd be playing the harpsichord and singing about hills. Every single bloody night, while feckless men with curly hair said things like "a marvellous recital, my dear" and "you have a most comely singing voice, Miss Jennifer" and "I do hear that Mr Gilliray has sent to London for new gaiters". There is *no way* I'm going back to that when there are jewels to rub on our faces and people to stab.'[10]

'Oh, I wouldn't worry,' said the albino pirate. 'The Pirate Captain is always giving up pirating. It's part of "the rich tapestry of life under his command", or so he says.'

'I've been with him for fifteen years,' said the grizzled pirate with skin like an old accordion,

---

10   In fact, as a Victorian Lady Jennifer would most likely be either dying in childbirth or setting fire to herself whilst cooking, the two most common forms of death amongst women back in the nineteenth century.

58

'and in that time he's given up pirating to become a fireman, a magician, a short-order chef, a Russian spy, a statue, an enigma and a circus strongman. And I'm senile, so I've probably forgotten dozens more.'

The pirate with a scarf leaned against the mast and stroked his rugged chin thoughtfully. 'I don't know. I think Jennifer might have a point. The Captain did a thing with his jaw this time that I've never seen before. I worry when he does new facial expressions. He normally only has three or four.'

'Come off it,' snorted the pirate in red. 'He doesn't know the first thing about bee-keeping; he literally doesn't know one end of a bee from the other.'

'Well, I don't want to leave things to chance,' said Jennifer. 'And I've got an idea. Because if I've learnt one thing about our Captain, it's that he tends to follow the path of least resistance.'

'That's true,' nodded the pirate in green.

'So, perhaps if pirating was made to *seem* a little easier, then he might forget all about this bee-keeping business.'

'How do you mean?'

'Right,' said Jennifer, leaning over to whisper into the pirate with a scarf's ear conspiratorially. 'Here's my plan.'

Jennifer burst into the Pirate Captain's cabin, waving a piece of old parchment that smelled faintly of tea and matches. The Captain, nose deep in a book, looked up in surprise.

'You'll never guess what just happened!' exclaimed Jennifer. 'Whilst you were busy down here an old dying pirate turned up on a raft! He was half mad with sunstroke, but just before he expired he gave us this map, and he said something about how there were a million doubloons buried in a secret cove, and he added that it would be really easy to find, and he promised that there'd be necklaces and emeralds and stuff like that. So, should I order the boys to change course?'

'Aaarr,' said the Pirate Captain, going back to his book with a shrug. 'You know how it is with treasure. It's bound to be guarded by a giant crab or undead skeletons or something. Best off sticking with the bees. Most of *their* adventures seem to consist of meeting up with friendly children and helping them out.'

Jennifer looked confused. The Pirate Captain held up his book, the cover of which showed a cute child with ringlets and a smiling bee on her finger. The title read *The Children's Golden Treasury of Bee Stories*.

'It's the absolute bible of all things bee-related,' said the Pirate Captain. 'It tells you all about how they live, but in the form of easily digested large-print stories with plenty of pictures. Look: here's one of a couple of bees sledging with a teddy bear. I imagine the bear's a bit fanciful, but the sledging looks about right. Clever little things, they are.'

'Are you sure that's not just a children's book?' said Jennifer.

'Absolutely. You see, it's very detailed about bee society, which it turns out is fascinating. The main threat to their livelihood seems to be grumpy grasshoppers.'

Half an hour later, Jennifer was back on deck, glumly telling the crew about the Pirate Captain's lengthy description of bee society and how, for the duration of the voyage to St Helena, he planned to run the boat along bee lines, with him as the King Bee, half the pirates as the worker bees, the other pirates as soldier bees and the cabin boys as grubs. He wanted to label all the ham as 'royal jelly' and have them feed it to him while he lay in his hammock not moving very much, apart from getting up from time to time to judge the quality of their waggle dancing. Much as they loved their Captain, none of the pirates were particularly keen on this idea.

'Look,' said the pirate in green after a bit more deliberation. 'I think I know what will work. How would you go about catching a mouse?'

'A big net!' said the pirate with a hook for a hand.

'Dress as a cat and chase it with a knife!' said the eye-candy pirate.

'Shrink to mouse size and hide under the mouse's bed and then when they fall asleep jump up and bundle them into a sack,' said the pirate with a squint.

'Or,' said the pirate in green, who was quite enjoying the chance to be the one with a scheme for a change, 'you could set a mousetrap. Which I mean in a metaphorical sense. We give the Pirate Captain some bait and wait for him to go for it.'

'Oh, for pity's sake! How is that any different to *my* plan?' asked Jennifer, exasperated. 'Honestly, you lot are all as bad as each other.'

Back in his cabin the Pirate Captain stared out of his porthole, contemplating whether to replace his luxuriant beard of glossy hair with a luxuriant beard of glossy bees. On balance he decided that whilst there would be obvious styling advantages, they might be a bit noisy to have on your chin all the time. His thoughts were interrupted by a rather unrealistic boat swinging into view outside the porthole. It floated oddly above the water for a few seconds, looking slightly two-dimensional, before a voice eventually piped up.

'What hard work it is on this Royal Navy boat,' said the voice. 'It is a great worry to us sailors that we are here without any cannons and all this gold.' The ship jiggled up and down. 'Oh yes. I hope no brave pirates come to get us because we're pretty poorly defended I can tell you, oh yes.'

Another voice sounded more muffled and said something like, 'Keep it still, you idiot! Mention the sails.'

'Oh woe,' said the first voice again. 'Here comes another boat. I hope it isn't pirates because as I said we're a sitting duck. What with our *sails* being missing too.'

A second boat swung in from the left. This one had a flag with a crude picture of a woman in a leotard drawn on it. 'Are you pirates?' said the first voice.

'No,' said a new voice, which was slightly more high-pitched. 'We are a boat full of Miss World contestants. We are looking for a pirate captain with a pleasant, open face. We would like to join his crew if at all possible. Do you know where we can find one?'

'We do not,' said the first voice. 'Thank the Queen, hoorah we don't.'

The two ships bobbed about for a bit, seemingly lost for words.

'Ooh! Pirates,' said the first voice.

'My arms are tired,' said the other voice. Then they started arguing about breakfast cereal.

The Pirate Captain didn't take it personally when the crew underestimated his intelligence, because he was the first to admit that there had been times when he'd proved less than perceptive. There was the birthday party where he had spent two hours trying to chat up a pile of coats, having mistaken them for Lola Montez. He had only recently found out that lambs were baby sheep, rather than a completely different species. And he still got eggs mixed up with tomatoes. Never the less, he thought it might be a good idea to have a chat with the men to set a few things straight. He closed his book, tucked a roll of fabric under his arm and strode up on deck, where the crew were huddled together

65

next to the mast. The Captain coughed discreetly.

'Wait! We're not ready!' said the pirate with encephalitis, who was the first to notice him.

'It's all right, lads,' said the Pirate Captain. 'I think we need to have a little talk.'

There was a frenzy of activity from the huddle of pirates, which then parted to reveal the pirate with a hook for a hand, who for some reason was wearing a greasy periwig, spectacles mended with a sticking plaster and an anorak, zipped up to the top.

'Hello, Pirate Captain,' said the pirate with a hook for a hand in a nasal voice. 'I hear you are famous for enjoying adventures in which you encounter notable historical characters. I am Charles Babbage and I'm trying to invent a mechanical engine that does sums, but an evil magpie has stolen all my cogs. Can you help me have an adventure to get them all back before greedy developers turn my orphanage into a death-ray factory?'

The Pirate Captain shook the pirate's hand, mainly because he was polite. 'I'm sorry, Mr

Babbage, but helping historical figures isn't really my line of work any more. I'm a bee-keeper now. We tend more towards sitting next to babbling brooks and indulging in quiet pastoral reflection, that kind of thing.'

The pirate with a hook for a hand looked disappointed. 'I think the magpie was working for Otto von Bismarck,' he added hopefully.

'What about me?' said a pirate in a tall top hat. 'I'm Isambard Kingdom Brunel and I'm being attacked by a sea monster.' He wrestled with a rubbery tentacle.

'Look, you scurvy knaves,' said the Pirate Captain as patiently as he could manage. 'You're not going to talk me out of this. I know what you're thinking: "If we can invent a scheme to convince the Pirate Captain that it's worth being a pirate again, he'll forget this whole bee-keeping business and go back to what he's best at. Bee-keeping is clearly a fad."'

'That's *sort* of what we thought,' said Jennifer sheepishly, 'except we described the bee-keeping as a "passing whimsy".'

'Basically, you're saying I'm fickle.'

'Just that you might be a bit better at starting projects than you are at following them through to a decent conclusion,' said the pirate in red with a shrug. 'It was only a month ago you got really into vivisection.' The pirate in green lifted up his shirt and pointed towards where he had a beak sewn a bit haphazardly onto his belly. 'But you seem to have forgotten all about that now.'

'That's because I hadn't found the right project. Bee-keeping is my one true love.'

The pirates stared sulkily at their shoes.

'Stop staring sulkily at your shoes and look up there instead,' said the Pirate Captain, pointing to the top of the main mast. 'What do you see?'

'A seagull!' said the pirate with asthma.

'The sun!' shouted the pirate who was now blind.

'Space! We're going into space! I can't wait!' said the albino pirate.

'A bit lower,' said the Pirate Captain.

'Worrying signs of dry rot?' said the pirate with long legs.

'No I mean the *flag*,' said the Pirate Captain. 'The skeleton and bones flag, which has another name that I can't remember right now, but that's not important. In the past, whenever I've adopted a new career, I've never taken it down. Not once. Hell's teeth, *most* of my previous vocations were chosen purely on the basis that I could keep the flag. Remember when I was a poison-maker? My osteopathy practice? The week I spent as a skeleton impersonator?'[11]

The Pirate Captain took the roll of fabric from under his arm and unfurled it. It was a flag, but instead of a skull and crossbones it showed the Pirate Captain sitting astride a bee, flying happily into a new future. The Captain smiled and flourished it at the crew. 'So to show you how serious I am about all this I want you to say hello to your new flag.'

'Why,' said the pirate in red, 'does it show you holding your crotch? Is that a bee-keeper thing?'

---

11 Pirates usually designed their own flags. It's a toss-up as to whether the best was Edward Teach's, which showed a demon stabbing a blood-red heart with a big spear, or Bartholomew Roberts', which showed a pirate having a friendly drink with a skeleton. But the worst was definitely Walter Kennedy's, who might have been a good pirate, but couldn't draw faces to save his life.

'I'm riding a bee,' explained the Pirate Captain. 'It's just you can't really see it because the bee is drawn to scale. Now come on, say "hello" to the flag. That wasn't just a figure of speech, it was an order, so hop to it before I keel-haul the lot of you.'

'Hello, flag,' said the pirates, waving without much enthusiasm.

'What do we call you now?' asked the pirate with a scarf, scratching his scar ruefully. 'The Bee-keeper Captain, I suppose?'

'Aaaaar, no. I'll be sticking with Pirate Captain. Because whilst I'm definitely a bee-keeper and there's no going back, I don't want to have to change my headed notepaper again.'

Five

HEROES OF THE
MYSTERY SHIPS

'I'm not much of a one for adjectives, number two, because I think they're a bit effeminate,' said the Pirate Captain, surveying the rain-lashed landscape stretched out behind the little bay where they had parked the pirate boat. 'I've always been more of a noun man. Good solid reliable nouns. Nouns don't mess you about. But if I *was* to use adjectives to describe this island they would probably be ones like: "bleak", "bare", "dismal", "exposed", "stark", "windswept", "treeless", "defoliated", "joyless" and "parky". Which is strange, because Black Bellamy's brochure makes quite a point of using adjectives like "lush", "verdant", "warm", "balmy", "luxuriant", "thriving", "idyllic", "Elysian" and "paradisiacal".'

'Which are almost the exact opposites!' exclaimed the albino pirate.

'Yes. It doesn't make sense,' said the Captain with a frown. 'He might not have a vocabulary to match mine, but I can't believe he'd get them all quite *that* wrong. Still, I'm sure there must be a perfectly good explanation. Maybe there's an eclipse or something,' he added hopefully, squinting up at the slate-grey sky. They trudged on a bit further up the shingle, but exotic parrots carried on failing to burst into colourful song, and winsome tropical ladies laden with garlands and ukuleles resolutely refused to pop out from behind the treeline. The only sign of life was a few miserable-looking goats, which shivered by some rocks and stared balefully back at the pirates.

'I don't like goats,' said the albino pirate. 'It's those strange alien eyes. They give me the creeps. Though I realise that's a bit pot-and-kettle.'

They'd almost made it to the top of a scraggy little hill when, through the relentless sheets of drizzle, the Pirate Captain suddenly made out a figure hurrying towards them.

'Oh, look,' he said, pointing. 'Here's a native. Quick, give me a bead or a comb, number two.'

The pirate with a scarf fished around in his pockets.

'I've got this old milk bottle top. Will that do?'

'Yes, that's the ticket.' The Captain nodded

towards the native, who was waving and getting a bit closer now. Poor chap is probably labouring under the idea that this is the land of his spirit ancestors or some rubbish like that. But not to worry. Because in my experience the great thing about indigenous populations is that if you give them something shiny they'll happily sell you their sister.'

The Captain drew himself up to his full height, and waved back at the native, who had almost reached them now and appeared a little out of breath.

'HELLO THERE. I'M THE PIRATE CAPTAIN,' said the Pirate Captain loudly, striding forward. He pressed the milk bottle top into the native's hand. 'PLEASE DON'T MISTAKE ME FOR A GOD. WE GOT IN ALL SORTS OF BOTHER THE LAST TIME THAT HAPPENED, AND FRANKLY THERE'S ONLY SO MUCH SACRIFICIAL LAMB'S BLOOD A FELLOW CAN DRINK. ANYWAY, HERE IS A SHINY MILK BOTTLE TOP. ALL THIS,' the Captain indicated the island with a sweep of his arm, 'MINE NOW. DO YOU HAVE A SISTER?'

The man blinked and looked confused. He was very well dressed for a native, thought the Pirate Captain. Usually they wore nothing at all, or, if you were lucky, they'd have gourds over their bits. But this one was wearing a nice warm duffel coat with a woolly hat pulled down around his ears, and he was carrying a sensible umbrella.[12]

'I'm not sure I really follow you,' said the native cheerily. 'But thank you very much for the bottle top.'

'PERHAPS YOU HAVE SOME KIND OF CHIEFTAIN'S HUT YOU COULD TAKE US TO? DON'T WORRY ABOUT HEFTING ME THERE ON YOUR SHOULDERS, WALKING IS FINE. IT'S JUST I'M QUITE KEEN TO GET OUT OF THIS RAIN BEFORE IT DOES SOMETHING TERRIBLE TO MY LUXURIANT BEARD.'

'Goodness me, of course,' said the native. 'You're hardly dressed for this weather. Come along.'

---

12 In eighteenth-century Britain, umbrellas were seen as an effeminate French affectation and if you went out in the rain with one, some urchins would shout, "Frenchman, Frenchman! Why don't you call a coach?"

The pirates followed him across a landscape that seemed to be made mostly out of puddles and more scrawny goats, until they arrived at a battered but neat-looking village. A small row of houses huddled together around what the pirate with a scarf supposed was meant to be the village green, but would more accurately be described as the village grey, or best of all, he couldn't help but think gloomily, not described at all.

'This isn't so bad,' said the Pirate Captain. 'I think I'll probably call it New Piratecaptainville. I was a bit worried it would be like our adventure with the Aztecs and all the buildings and furniture would turn out to be made of hearts.'

'Oh no, there's nothing like that,' laughed the native, ushering the pirates through the door of one of the houses and into an oak-panelled hallway.

'You laugh, but to be fair it's surprisingly comfortable, waking up on a pillow of ventricles. Sticky though.'

'Yes, I can imagine.' The native took the pirates' sodden hats and coats and went on looking a bit bewildered. 'Now then. There's a nice log fire in the study, if you want to warm yourselves up. I'll just get some tea. I say tea, it's more a sort of seaweed–saltwater infusion, because it's rather hard to get hold of tea all the way out here. We did have a packet of digestives, but I'm afraid they ran out, and it's another six months before the next supply boat. I'm sorry I can't offer you more. It's not often we have visitors, you see.'

The native smiled. One of the pirates sneezed.

'Aaarrr,' said the Pirate Captain, giving the pirate a cuff around the head. 'Here's this fellow, being so polite, and with that one sneeze you've probably doomed the entire population of this island. Because they're not used to our germs.' The Pirate Captain turned back to the native and pulled a guilty face. 'Sorry about that, I do hope you won't have too lingering a death.'

'Dear me, no,' agreed the native, handing the pirates towels so they could dry themselves off.

78

'So, how can I help you?' asked the native, once he'd returned with a tray of murky tea.

The Pirate Captain pulled out the deeds that Black Bellamy had given him.

'The fact is I'm now the legal owner of this island.' The Captain spread the deeds out on the study's table. 'I think you'll find these explain everything.'

The native squinted at the deeds for a minute. Then he squinted at the pirates and looked uncomfortable.

'I've come here to raise bees,' added the Captain helpfully. 'I've heard you're famous for your bees.'

'In a way we are,' said the native. 'In so much as St Helena has some of the thinnest, rattiest bees in the world.' He smiled again nervously. 'Look, I don't really know how to put this,' he added after a couple of awkward moments ticked by. 'But I'm afraid these deeds are a forgery.'

'A forgery?' repeated the Pirate Captain, his heart sinking into his shiny black boots. 'But Black Bellamy gave me his solemn piratical word!'

'What makes you think they're a forgery?' asked Jennifer.

'Well, young lady, if you study them closely, you'll see that the picture of the Queen's head is really quite badly drawn. And, if I'm not mistaken, this wax seal is actually the casing from a novelty cheese. Also, if you take the first letter of each sentence it spells out "Got you again, love BB". Plus the whole thing appears to be written on the back of the drinks menu from somewhere called The Skull Island Paradise Tiki Bar.'

The pirate crew did a uniformly poor job of not looking delighted at the news. The Pirate Captain slumped into the armchair and pulled a face.

'St Helena belongs to the British Empire. I'm the Governor, you see. I realise it's not quite as famous as some of the other colonies, like India or Canada or Australia, and that you can pretty much throw a stone across the length of the entire island, and that we're mostly only notable for having the largest species of earwig in the world,[13] but it's still a terribly important responsibility.'

---

13 *Labidura herculeana*, not seen alive since 1967, grew up to 3.3 inches long, twice the size of a *Megachile pluto*.

'Pish,' said the Pirate Captain, because he couldn't think of anything more piratical to say. 'That's a bit of a blow.'

'Forgive me for appearing to think the worst of people, but is it possible this Black Bellamy character might have been playing a trick on you?'

'Truth be told,' said the pirate with a scarf, 'it wouldn't *exactly* be the first time.'

'Hey ho,' said Jennifer, trying not to beam too much. 'Them's the breaks. I suppose it's back to the sea for us. Thank you very much for the tea.'

Several of the pirates made to get up, but the Pirate Captain waved for them to sit down again. 'Not so fast, you scurvy lot.' He shot them an admonishing waggle of his eyebrows, and beckoned the Governor over to one side.

'Listen, Governor,' he said. 'Just between us men, this leaves me in a bit of a fix. You see, the lads have been really excited about becoming bee-keepers, and I hate to disappoint them. So what if I made it three bottle tops, and threw in one of my more expendable pirates? That chap over there in red, he's a good hard worker.' The Captain did his most winning smile.

'I don't think Her Majesty really exchanges pieces of her empire for bottle tops,' said the Governor.

'Aarrrr,' said the Captain. 'But look at their eager little faces.' He indicated the row of pirate faces. 'And those big eyes. They'd be heartbroken.'

'Well,' said the Governor, pondering for a moment. 'They *do* have big eyes. And I suppose there *is* old Mrs Blystone's place. She passed away recently. Eaten by goats. Sad business. It's not a very spacious house I'm afraid, and the roof leaks rather, but you could stay there if you like. After all, the island doesn't have a bee-keeper[14] at present, so you'd be a welcome addition to the local economy.'

'Any chance of arranging some sort of commemorative stamp with my face on it, just for appearances' sake?'

---

14 According to *The Bee-Master of Warrilow* (Tickner Edwards, 1907), bee-keepers come in three varieties: ruthless businessmen, the hidebound 'old school' who hate progress and 'reserved, silent men, difficult to approach' who grew up amongst the hives and, 'in the right circumstances, make the most charming of companions'.

'We do tend to stick to Queen Victoria's face, Captain. Sorry.'

'Fair enough. No harm in asking.'

The Pirate Captain, who was starting to impress himself with his new-found and frankly uncharacteristic firmness of purpose, turned to his pirates and they looked expectantly back at him.

'Unpack the boat, lads,' he roared, banging his cup of tea down on the mantelpiece, because banging things was always his favourite way of illustrating those moments when he made a particularly important decision. 'We're staying!'

The pirates all seemed to deflate where they were sitting, like a row of pirate-shaped balloons.

'Come on, don't all look so dour. And if it helps to get you to turn those frowns upside down,' he added, 'then try to think of this as a very long, uneventful adventure on an exotic island. You know, like in that Robinson Crusoe book. But with better hats, and less narrative thrust.'

Six

SEVENTEEN WAYS TO
BREAK MY HEART

'You've got the canapés ready?' asked the Pirate Captain, anxiously straightening his beard ribbons in the hallway mirror of their new home.

'Yes, Captain,' said the pirate with a scarf. 'And I've made the napkins into little swans like you wanted.'

'Good man. I want your buckles at their most shiny and your scarves to be at their jauntiest, because this housewarming party is the perfect opportunity for us to make a big social splash.'

Even though they suspected that 'making a big social splash' wasn't half as much fun as 'making a big actual splash in the sea with cannonballs', the pirates dutifully went about the task of tidying up the living room in preparation for the housewarming party. They found that pretending dust was Black Bellamy's crew helped with the dusting, and that pretending spoons were the sexier bits of mermaids helped with the polishing.

'It's incredibly important that we make a good first impression,' continued the Pirate Captain. 'I really can't emphasise that enough. It's just like with chimpanzees, you see.'

'I'm not sure I follow, Captain,' said the pirate with a scarf, carefully putting out the best china.

'Social hierarchies,' explained the Captain, who had once taken a primatology course at Pirate Academy for extra credit. 'You see, when a new chimpanzee joins a group of other chimpanzees, the very first thing he has to do is make sure everybody realises that he's the Alpha Male. Of course, in chimpanzee circles he'll tend to do this by bashing a few baby chimps to bits against a tree, or punching some macaques.'

'Are you going to punch some macaques?' said the albino pirate hopefully.

'Unfortunately, as I learnt the hard way, it turns out you've got to be a bit more subtle than that in human circles. On account of our years of extra evolving. Social dominance amongst landlubbers is mainly established through throwing lavish parties and telling amazing anecdotes.'[15]

---

15 If you're hosting a party try to make sure you have plenty of biscuits. Custard creams recently topped a poll to find Britain's favourite biscuit, easily beating the competition with 93 per cent of the vote.

The Captain flicked open the catches on an old treasure chest and swung back the lid. He sifted through the piles of old socks and sandwiches and very carefully lifted out a small crystal bear.

'You know what this is?' he asked the pirate with a scarf, grinning.

'It's your crystal bear, sir.'

'No, number two, it's a *conversation piece*. A conversation piece is an old pirate trick. I'll put the crystal bear on the coffee table, and then guests will be bound to comment, giving me an opportunity to tell them an exciting story about how I came by it.'

'That's very clever, Captain. But didn't you get it from that shop on Oxford Street? The one that's full of crystal animal tat? The albino pirate cried when you wouldn't buy him a crystal unicorn. It's not much of an anecdote, to be honest.'

'Well, yes, that's as may be,' said the Captain. 'But our guests won't know that, will they? This is one of the best things about starting a new life abroad, you can make all sorts up about your past.' He tapped the side of his nose conspiratorially. 'I'll probably tell them that I won it in a game of poker with the Devil.'

One by one the islanders began to arrive, and the pirates all did their best to engage in pleasant small talk, and tried not to limit their conversation to the usual rather insular topics of treasure and types of rope. The pirate with an accordion played mood music, and the pirate with long legs made sure that everybody had enough jellyfish to eat, because boiled jellyfish, rain and pebbles seemed to be pretty much all the island had to offer in the way of cuisine. Very soon the Pirate Captain had quite a crowd gathered round him, hanging on his every word.

'Here's an interesting fact,' he said, winking at a particularly gamine lady islander, perching on his knee with an adoring look in her eye. 'We had an adventure with Charles Darwin a little while ago, and according to his theories a small, isolated population such as yourselves will probably mutate into fish people within a few generations.'

'Really?' said the gamine lady islander. 'How fascinating! And you've met such interesting people! We must seem terribly dull in comparison.'

'Aarrr, not at all. I think you'd look good with gills, by the way.'

'Oh, you're such a charmer, Pirate Captain.'

'I am, but there's much more to me than the charming rogue who plunders stuff and sets fire to things. I'm also surprisingly spiritual.'

'I like spiritual things!'

'I could tell. Now, for instance, a while back I stole a whole lot of gold Buddhas from some Tibetan monks. Can't get more spiritual than that.'

'What a life you've led,' sighed the girl. 'You're easily the most famous and exciting person to have ever visited St Helena.'

The Pirate Captain turned his grin to full beam. 'I suppose I must be.'

'I like your crystal bear, by the way.'

'Ah, as it happens there's an interesting story behind that. 1812, it must have been.' The Captain spoke extra loud to make sure he had everybody's attention. 'Me and my loyal manservant Pappaganeo were on an expedition to find the source of the Amazon, with just a battered canoe made out of old tiger skins . . .'

But before the Pirate Captain could get any further into his anecdote there was a sudden loud knock at the door. All the pirates jumped, because they weren't used to the fact that on land people could just turn up unannounced and knock at your door. The only things that tended to turn up unannounced at sea were bouts of dysentery and the occasional albatross.

'Goodness me!' exclaimed the Governor. 'Who can this be? Another visitor in the space of a day?'

'Maybe it's the Pirate King come to try to persuade the Pirate Captain to go back to pirating,' said Jennifer hopefully.

'Maybe it's Black Bellamy come to apologise for the earlier mix-up,' said the pirate who was quite naïve.

'No, look!' said the pirate in green peering out the window. 'It's the Royal Navy! They've come to arrest us! We'll be hung in irons!'

'Why would they arrest law-abiding bee-keepers?' pointed out the Captain, with a roll of his eyes. He excused himself from the gamine lady and the throng of islanders and went to open the door. A young naval officer carrying a clipboard looked him up and down.

'Is this St Helena?' he asked, frowning.

'That's right,' said the Pirate Captain. 'Can I help?'

'Delivery for you.' The naval officer held out his clipboard. 'Sign here. No, not there, here, where I've put a little X. Right.' He snapped his fingers and from behind him two burly sailors appeared, flanking a chained figure in a long military coat and a distinctive peaked hat. They unshackled their prisoner, handed him a suit-case and then, with a sharp salute, they and the officer disappeared back down towards the direction of the beach, leaving the man on his own. He peered about his new surroundings with a barely concealed look of disdain. The

93

islanders all seemed rooted to the spot, so the Pirate Captain, deciding it was only right to be polite, strode forward and proffered his hand.

'Hello,' he said. 'Welcome to St Helena. I'm the Pirate Captain, the island's most famous resident. Goodness me, you look terribly familiar.'

'I imagine I do,' said the man.

'Don't tell me.' The Captain clicked his tongue thoughtfully. 'Have you ever advertised fish fingers?'

'Certainly not.'

'Modelled for erotic etchings?'

'No.'

'Ah, I've got it – the steak counter at the butcher's on Cowley Road in Oxford!'

The man shook his head once more.

'Oh well, I give up. But I could swear I know you from somewhere. Though maybe you've just got one of those faces that looks like everybody else's face. Some people have those. They've done scientific studies on it.'

The man doffed his hat and bowed. 'Behold Napoleon!' he exclaimed. 'Unjustly deposed

Emperor of the French, King of Italy, Mediator of the Swiss Confederation and Protector of the Confederation of the Rhine!'

'Aarrrrr,' said the Pirate Captain, a little flustered. He bowed back, because he couldn't think of what else to do in the circumstances. 'Well, behold me. Bronze swimming certificate. Owner of several hats. Protector of, um, some bees.'

Everybody, pirates and islanders alike, gaped at the new arrival.

'Now listen here.' Napoleon picked up his suitcase, stalked into the room, grasped the Pirate Captain's shoulder and fixed him with a serious stare. 'It is usual when meeting me for the first time that men question the very worth of their lives. I know how your thoughts must be running at the moment. "My goodness!" you think. "Here is a man, if such a word does him justice, which frankly it doesn't, who has conquered most of the world! Who has set himself amongst the gods! My life appears so trivial in comparison!" But try not to think those thoughts, because that way only madness lies. You should not judge yourself by Napoleon's incomparable standards. Just as you would not judge, say, an ant, or some sort of rodent, by your own. Besides, in many ways I'm sure your trivial achievements are just as important as my gargantuan ones.' Napoleon paused and stared nobly into the middle distance. 'Because ultimately I am a man, just like you. And I want you to treat me like an equal, ridiculous though that must seem.'

With that, Napoleon gave the Pirate Captain a big Gallic hug, and then spun on his heel to survey the rest of the room. Noticing Jennifer, he doffed his hat again and stepped forward to kiss her hand.

'Young lady, *enchanté*,' said Napoleon. 'Do not be surprised or embarrassed if you swoon in my presence. It is quite the normal reaction amongst the fairer sex.'

'I'll do my best,' said Jennifer.

'And you.' Napoleon patted the pirate with a scarf on the back. 'You too are probably feeling you will faint just from the thrill of breathing the same air as Napoleon. Well, faint away! Nobody will think any less of you.'

The pirate with a scarf just blushed and stared at the floor.

'Shouldn't you be off trying to take over the world, Mister Napoleon?' asked the albino pirate, looking a bit star-struck. 'Or have you changed jobs and become a bee-keeper too?'

'No, my porcelain friend,' said Napoleon, his face suddenly clouding over. 'I simply grew tired of the conquering business. So I have come here to this godforsaken rock to enjoy a peaceful retirement. I am here completely of my own volition, and anybody who says otherwise is a liar and a charlatan.'

'Mister Bonaparte,' said the Governor, hurrying forward to take the general's things. 'It's a real honour to have you as a guest on our humble island.'

'Anyhow,' said the Pirate Captain, turning back to the gamine lady islander, having decided it was high time he got his anecdote back on track. 'As I was saying, there's a rather interesting story behind how I came by that crystal bear.'

'Ah yes, *bears*,' said Napoleon. He nimbly slipped his arm around the gamine girl's waist

97

and led her over to a couch. 'That reminds me of the time I invaded Russia. Let me tell you all about it. You are extremely gamine, by the way.'

Across the room Jennifer leaned over to the pirate with a scarf. 'The Pirate Captain's gone a very funny colour,' she said. 'What on earth can the matter be?'

'I think,' replied the pirate with a scarf ruefully, 'it has something to do with chimpanzees.'

Seven

DATELINE: MURDERING!

'What a ridiculous little man,' remarked the Pirate Captain to nobody in particular over breakfast the next morning. 'Have you ever met anyone with such a high opinion of themselves?'

'It rings a bell,' said the pirate in red.

'It's a wonder his head doesn't explode,' said the Pirate Captain, choosing to ignore this comment. 'Remind me not to wear my best coat when I'm around the fellow, because I don't want to end up with exploding Corsican brain goo all over me.'

'Well, I think it's very exciting to have Mister Napoleon as a neighbour,' said the albino pirate. 'I mean to say, he almost conquered the whole of Europe!'

'And I ate the whole of that mixed grill that time. Not "almost ate", you'll notice. I finished the job,' said the Captain with a scowl, moodily buttering his Weetabix.

At the sound of an envelope plopping onto the mat, all the pirates bounded excitedly to the door. In comparison to the sort of sounds that got the pirates excited on their previous adventures 'the sound of an envelope plopping onto the mat' wasn't really all that great. Normally they could expect 'the sound of grapeshot tearing through the rigging' or 'the sound of a tidal wave crashing across the deck' or at the very least 'the sound of the pirate in green being a bit seasick'. But with their new domestic existence they found they had to settle for what they could get.

'An envelope!' said the albino pirate. 'What do you suppose it could be?'

'Maybe it's a love letter from an admiral's daughter!'

'Or a chain letter telling us we'll get cursed if we don't pass it on to five people we know, in which case we should ignore it, because chain letters are a form of bullying.'

'Maybe we've won some premium bonds!'

The pirates went on discussing what the letter could be for a while, until the Pirate Captain strode over from the breakfast table and picked it up with a flourish.

'Never occurs to you lot to just *open* something, does it?' he said, shaking his head in exasperation. 'We do have cutlasses for a reason, you know.'

The Pirate Captain slit open the envelope, and pulled out an embossed square of paper. It read:

YOU ARE CORDIALLY INVITED TO AN
IMPROMPTU LITTLE GATHERING

AT THE HOUSE OF NAPOLEON BONAPARTE,
ST HELENA'S NEW MOST
FAMOUS RESIDENT

RSVP

'Wow, that's a fancy invitation!' exclaimed the pirate with long legs. 'Look, he's done all raised lettering. And feel how thick the paper is that it's printed on! It must be at least 150gsm!'

'It certainly makes those invitations you sent out written on bits of seaweed look a bit poor, doesn't it, Pirate Captain?' said the pirate who liked kittens and sunsets.

The Captain's beard shook in a way that the pirates recognised signified either trouble or the presence of an approaching typhoon, and for a moment he seemed lost for words. Eventually he found his tongue. 'He can't throw a house-warming party the very day after I've thrown a housewarming party! It's against all known social etiquette. The cheek of the man!'

'Is Napoleon your new nemesis, Pirate Captain?' asked the pirate in green, who liked to try and keep track of these kind of things.

'At this rate I think he might very well be. But not the good kind of nemesis like Black Bellamy, who you have a grudging respect for. He's the terrible kind who just gets on your nerves.' The Captain glowered. 'And do you know what the worst thing is?'

'Ooh, I do!' said the pirate with gout, putting up his hand. 'It's unrequited love. You know, when a girl with hazel eyes and flaxen hair who's your whole reason for living hardly even notices you exist. That's the worst thing ever.'

'Yes, true enough, but the worst thing at *this* particular moment is that I don't have a thing to wear. Come on, number two, let's see if we can wash some of that octopus ink out of my spare blousy shirt.'

'Is this what our life is going to entail now?' asked Jennifer glumly. 'An endless series of polite dinner parties?'

'That dead jellyfish you served at your party was lovely, Pirate Captain,' said Napoleon, bringing in a big plate to the dining table where the pirates, the Governor and the rest of the islanders were gathered. 'I hope this small selection of sweetmeats, stuffed artichokes, pressed quail's eggs and caviar, brought with me from the finest Paris delicatessen, will live up to your exacting standards.'

Everybody tucked eagerly into their food, the pirates because they always tucked eagerly into anything put in front of them, and the islanders because it was clearly years since any of them had eaten something that wasn't the colour and texture of old flannels.

'I like your wallpaper, Mister Napoleon,' said the pirate in green, through a mouthful of duck livers.

'Yes, it is nice, isn't it?' said Napoleon, taking a seat and lighting an expensive-looking cigar. 'A gift from the British, to show that there were no hard feelings.'

The Pirate Captain leaned over to the pirate with a scarf. 'You see what he's doing?' he whispered.

'Being a consummate host?'

'He's trying to show me up. "Impromptu little gathering" my hat. Look, he's even stolen that swan napkin idea of mine.'

'I don't think you invented folding napkins into animal shapes, Captain.'

'So, let me get this straight,' said Jennifer, who was frowning in a pretty way. 'St Helena doesn't have any volcanoes, cannibals, smugglers or sinister Prussians. What does that leave? Ghosts? You must have a ghost?'

'I'm afraid not, my dear,' said the Governor.

'Not even one?'

'Well . . .' The Governor chewed thoughtfully for a few moments. 'We did have a rock that several of the islanders thought looked a *bit* like a ghost. But it fell into the sea, ooh, at least ten years ago.'

Jennifer slumped, in as much as she could slump, because as a Victorian lady she had naturally good posture at all times.

'You may be interested to know that *I* have had an encounter with the supernatural realm,' said Napoleon, patting Jennifer's hand, his eyes gleaming. At the other end of the table the Pirate Captain made a groaning noise, but the little general did not appear to notice.

'Go on,' said Jennifer eagerly.

'It was during my invasion of Northern Italy. We were marching through deep snow by the light of the moon, a terrible blizzard blowing up around us. Eventually it got so bad that I decided we must stop and find shelter. By luck, the blizzard slowed for just a moment and we caught sight of a small village up ahead. The peasant shacks were dark and forbidding and even I, Napoleon, felt a shiver of apprehension as we approached.'

One of the younger pirates began to suck their thumb nervously. Napoleon leaned forward and continued. 'Despite the bitter weather, outside each hut huddled a peasant family, looking back at us with dim, idiot eyes. I demanded that they bring us food and fresh horses, but they just stood there. So I grew angry and fired my pistol into the air, but still there was no response. It was as if they were statues!'

'Dear me, are you scared of *statues*?' asked the Pirate Captain. 'Is it because they look like people but actually they're made out of stone?'

'I hadn't finished,' said Napoleon. 'Anyway, to cut a long story short it turned out that all the peasants were werewolves and so we shot them with cannons.' He leaned back in his chair and grinned. 'Pretty spooky stuff, eh?'

Most of the pirates and islanders agreed that it was a very scary story and they couldn't imagine anything more frightening. The Pirate Captain stifled a yawn. 'I suppose werewolves are *fairly* spooky,' he said.

'I didn't know you'd ever met werewolves!' exclaimed Jennifer.

'Oh yes. We had bucketloads of adventures with werewolves back in the day. So many, in fact, I'd almost forgotten that some people find them terrifying.'

'Surely,' said the Governor, who had now turned quite white, 'you're not suggesting that you've met something more spooky than a were-wolf, Pirate Captain?'

'Most days. An obvious example that springs to mind is the adventure where we were search-ing for some mythical Olmec gold. Sailed all over the place looking for it. Tricky customers those Olmecs, they have a tendency to stash their treasure in really inconvenient and unex-pected places. We ended up at a haunted house in Raynes Park. Do you know Raynes Park?'

The islanders fell into an animated discus-sion, but none of them had heard of Raynes Park. Napoleon sat with his arms folded and made a face.

'It's a suburb just south of London,' explained the Pirate Captain helpfully, 'between Wimble-don and New Malden. It's not *that* eldritch a place to be honest, but this particular haunted house was really awful . . . you know, holes in the roof, bats, glow-in-the-dark stuff hanging off the trees in the garden. We could hear a blood-curdling noise coming from the attic, so me and the lads knocked down the door and crept up the stairs, which were all creaky like you'd expect. Ghosts are notoriously lax at house repairs. I assume it's because when you're dead it wouldn't seem that important, would it? Stands to reason. Anyhow, as we got onto the landing, the noises became louder and even more sinister. But bold as brass I gripped my cutlass and marched straight up to the little attic ladder, expecting monsters. Sure enough, there were a load of them in there, making a horrible racket. Monsters! And they were sat round a table *just like this one*.' The Pirate Captain lowered his voice eerily. 'But where you're sitting,' he pointed at the islanders in turn, 'was a zombie! And where you're sitting was a dracula! And in your place was a triffid and next to you was a Creature from the Black Lagoon! And, Governor, in your seat there was a painting where the eyes follow you about the room!'

The Governor put his hand to his mouth and let out a stifled shriek.

'And where you're sitting,' said the Pirate Captain, looking directly at Napoleon, 'there was a little chubby maggot. Imagine that! I'll bet none of you have ever heard of anything so spine-chilling.'

Napoleon began to say that in fact he had just remembered an even more shocking and dreadful story, but the Pirate Captain held up his hands to cut him off. 'Listen, Napoleon,' he said. 'I'm sure we could spend all night telling stories about how brave we are. But I'm a man of action, not words. So what do you say to a little contest?'

'What did you have in mind?' asked Napoleon, his eyes narrowing

'Well,' said the Captain, 'I was thinking along the lines of a "Draw a Monster" competition. We get some paper and pens and each of us draws something scary. The winner is the one who scares the other one most. If both of us are equally scared, then we'll try them on the Governor here.'

The Governor didn't look too happy about this. 'It's getting very late, Pirate Captain.

Perhaps it would be best if we all shake hands and get off to bed?'

'No!' exclaimed Napoleon. 'Let it never be said that Napoleon evades a worthy challenge. Please fetch some paper and pens from my desk.'

The Governor reluctantly went to get the required stationery while Napoleon flexed his drawing hand and the Pirate Captain ran through a few quick stretches. He was hoping Jennifer might offer to massage his shoulders and mentioned a few times how tense they were, but she didn't seem to take the hint.[16]

'Gentlemen,' said the Governor, once everybody was ready. 'You have twenty minutes to draw a monster. I'd rather we were all good sports and didn't copy or try to distract the other competitor. Your time starts now!'

Before putting pen to paper, the Pirate Captain decided that he needed a strategy. He didn't know Napoleon very well, but he realised that he had to somehow get under the French Emperor's

---

16 Things don't always go smoothly with girls. Famously, when Napoleon first tried to make love to Josephine he was bitten on his leg by her pug.

skin, to work out what made him tick and, most importantly, to discover what would terrify him out of his wits. 'If I was in his place,' thought the Pirate Captain, 'what would frighten me? I've always been a keen amateur psychologist, this should be easy enough.' Then the Pirate Captain remembered that he had often felt like he might be psychic, on account of the many bizarre and unexplainable things that had happened to him, such as the time when he found out he had the *exact same* birthday as a total stranger he once met on holiday.[17] With a psychic brain like that, he could probably just extract Napoleon's greatest fears through telepathy. He put one finger on each temple and stared at the back of Napoleon's head, which is where he assumed the frightening stuff was kept.

'What are you doing?' whispered Jennifer. 'Why have you gone cross-eyed? Are you ill? Was it last night's jellyfish? I still say we should try frying them instead of boiling.'

---

17 If you are in a room with only 23 people there is a 50 per cent chance that one of them shares your birthday.

'Shh . . . I'm sucking Napoleon's greatest fear out of his head with my mind powers.'

'Mind powers? When did you get those?'

'I don't know. I'm probably a mutant or descended from Gypsies. Do you mind being quiet?'

Jennifer apologised and left the Pirate Captain to it. She thought of sneaking a look at Napoleon's picture, but he had covered it with his arm so that nobody could see.

The Pirate Captain rapidly came to realise that psychic powers were much harder to use than he had expected. And with only a few minutes left he wondered whether he might be better off letting his powers flow through his pen. This worked slightly better, and before long he had drawn a monster with eight or nine googly eyes, tentacles, plenty of fangs and scales rather than skin. There was no time to colour it in, but the Captain figured that a monster might be scarier in black and white because it was 'stark'. Just as the Governor was telling them to put their pens down, he quickly sketched a few more heads – a dragon, a cat and a hen – sat back and folded his arms.

'Gentleman, if you could reveal your monsters,' said the Governor, a serious look on his face. The Pirate Captain pushed his picture forward as boldly as he could.

'There you go,' he said. 'I'm afraid it hasn't got a name.'

Seeing the Captain's drawing Napoleon suddenly screwed his sheet of paper into a ball and, with a sort of strangulated yelp, flung it into the Governor's fireplace. Then he sat back and mopped his brow.

'What on earth are you doing?' asked the Captain, shocked.

'I am sorry, Pirate Captain,' said Napoleon, shaking his head and suppressing a shudder. 'But my picture was so terrifying that had anyone other than I, Napoleon, looked upon the thing, it would have caused *their hearts to explode*. That's how scary it was. It's almost as if my skill as a draughtsman had actually summoned a demon from the occult realm.'

Several of the assembled islanders 'oohed' and 'aahed' at this.

'Well then,' said the Governor. 'I suppose we

must declare Napoleon the winner. For though your picture is very good, Captain, it hasn't made anybody's heart explode, thank the stars.'

'Don't feel bad, my friend,' added Napoleon consolingly. 'It is only because of my iron constitution that I was able to withstand it myself. More quail's eggs?'

Eight

SNAKES AMOK!

Most of the pirates were in the kitchen having afternoon tea. Some of them were balancing pieces of toast on top of each other, because they'd discovered that balancing things was one of the very few perks about being on dry land. The rest were taking it in turns to heave heavy sighs.

'Oh, come on, lads. You know I don't usually object to a bit of theatrical sighing, but it's getting quite tricky to read my newspaper.' The Captain waved his copy of the *St Helena Gazette* at them. 'You keep blowing the comics section away.'

'Sorry, Pirate Captain,' said the pirate in green, who was absent-mindedly carving a little picture of a starfish into the kitchen table. 'It's just, I think we're all missing the piratical life.'

'Not this again. If it really means that much to you we can always go and pirate some rocks or moss or something,' said the Pirate Captain magnanimously.

'It's not the same on dry land,' muttered the pirate with a nut allergy. 'Without the romance of the sea, pirating just seems like quite antisocial behaviour.'

'If you go about with that kind of negative attitude then of *course* everything looks grim. You have to try to see the natural beauty in things.' The Captain pointed out the window, towards where two goats were stood shivering on a grassy knoll. 'Look, over there. Those two goats. Clearly very much in love with each other. Doesn't that touch your soul?'

A few of the pirates peered at where the Captain was pointing.

'Why is the big goat biting the other goat on the thigh?' asked the albino pirate.

'It's an affectionate love bite,' the Captain explained.

'Oh! Now the little goat has responded by trying to hit the first goat round the head with a hoof,' said Jennifer.

'He's stroking her. That's a goat caress,' persisted the Captain.

'And now a whole load of other goats have joined in. It looks a lot like a fight.'

'It's a party. They're exuberant creatures.'

'Oh look, they've eaten the first goat now, Captain. There's just a skeleton left.'

'My point still stands,' said the Captain, forgetting what his point had been.

With a spray of rain and a gust of wind the cottage door swung open and in tramped two extremely dejected-looking pirates. After fighting for a few moments to close the door behind them, the pirate in green and the pirate with asthma stood shivering and looking like their world had ended. The pirate with asthma was crying.

'What's the matter, lads?' asked the Pirate Captain, sensing something was wrong. He prided himself on his ability to pick up on the moods of his crew, no matter how subtle the clues.

'Can you imagine a boring museum, Pirate Captain?' sniffed the pirate in green, sitting down miserably.

'It's difficult,' replied the Captain. All his experiences in museums had involved the exhibits being either cursed, mysterious or really educational. It seemed unlikely that any museum could be boring.

'Well, there's one right here on this island,' said the pirate with asthma through his tears. 'It wasn't exciting, there weren't any adventures and we didn't learn anything. And you know how much we love learning!' He sniffed noisily and blew his nose on his sleeve.

The Pirate Captain nodded and handed him a tissue. He *did* know how much the crew loved learning. The pirate in green continued. 'Most of the exhibits are just rubbish that you can find on the beach and the shop only sells leaflets and pens that don't work.' He showed the Pirate Captain a little pen with 'The National Museum of Antiquities and Natural History, St Helena' written down the side in wobbly handwriting.

'But surely there was something worth seeing?' said the Pirate Captain encouragingly. 'It's like I've just been explaining to the rest of the lads: try to concentrate on the positives.'[18]

'There *is* one of Mister Napoleon's handkerchiefs,' said the pirate with asthma, brightening up a bit. 'He was just donating it to the museum as we got there, which was very good of him. It's

---

18 There are actually quite a few boring museums you can visit around the world. Prague Castle has one that focuses almost exclusively on stone column bases.

on a plinth in a big jar of formaldehyde and there's a label explaining that it was the actual handkerchief he had in his pocket at the victory of Arcola, where he joined his infantry in a bayonet charge. That was quite interesting, I suppose.'

'Dear me. It *does* sound like a terrible museum,' said the Pirate Captain. He paused to take a couple of thoughtful sips of his tea. 'And, you know, as a responsible member of society I feel a certain obligation to help out.'

'You're noble like that,' nodded the albino pirate.

'I am. So, come on, lads, let's have a look through the treasure for something good to donate.'

Pretty soon the cottage was a mess of upended treasure chests, their contents strewn about the floor. Most of the treasure turned out to be straw, but there were also some sweet wrappers and a few dead rats.

'It's not looking very promising, is it, Captain?' said the pirate with a scarf, holding up an old, slightly petrified lamb chop.

The Pirate Captain sat amongst the mess for a few moments, at a bit of a loss. Then he looked up at the pirate with long legs and a wily look crept across his face. Several of the pirates got quite excited, because 'wily looks' tended to prefigure 'sticky situations'.

'How much would you say you weighed?' asked the Pirate Captain.

Not long after, the Captain was knocking at the museum door, whilst two of his crew struggled with a heavy-looking bundle wrapped up in some sacking. There was the sound of running feet and eventually the Governor appeared, wearing a peaked cap with 'Curator' written across the band.

'Pirate Captain! Hello!' said the Governor. 'Here to visit our national museum?'

'I am, yes,' said the Captain, beaming. 'Always been a big fan of this kind of cultural thing. Perhaps you could give me a little tour?'

The pirates hadn't been exaggerating about the museum. It was dark and damp, and smelled mostly of fish guts. The Governor was obviously so pleased to have a visitor that the Pirate Captain felt obliged to smile and make intelligent comments, but there were only so many things you could say about a collection of two thousand carefully catalogued pieces of driftwood, though he did manage to remark that the display of dead birds made him 'think about mortality'. The Governor got most excited when they reached a series of miniature dioramas.

'And this . . .' the Governor said proudly, 'is the prehistory of the island.' He pointed at a model of St Helena covered in a lush tropical jungle with sparkling waterfalls and trees heavy with exotic fruit. A couple of dinosaurs were standing next to a flag pole saluting the Union Jack.

'That was *this* island?' said the Pirate Captain, incredulous. 'What happened to all the plants?'

The Governor pointed at the next diorama, which featured a boat stuck on some rocks with a goat peeping out of a porthole. 'In 1567, a ship carrying the King of Spain's goats ran aground on the island. Two years later . . .' he ushered the Pirate Captain on to the next diorama, 'this was all that was left.' It showed the familiar windswept scenery, complete with a couple of goats looking moody as they polished off a dinosaur skeleton. Only the Union Jack remained.

'Bad news, those goats,' said the Pirate Captain. He patted the Governor on the shoulder.

'England will prevail, Pirate Captain. England will prevail. And finally, we have our star exhibit, as donated by our most celebrated islander, Mister Napoleon Bonaparte.'[19]

'Ah, yes, well, as a matter of fact, Curator, I'm in a bit of a hurry,' said the Pirate Captain, suddenly clapping his hands. 'So I suppose I ought to present you with *my* generous donation.'

'A donation? For us?' exclaimed the Governor.

---

19   The late John K. Lattimer, Professor Emeritus and former Chairman of Urology at the Columbia University College of Physicians and Surgeons, bought Napoleon's penis for $3,000 in an auction in 1977. It had previously been on display at the Museum of French Art.

'Seems only right that a man of my stature should help patronise such an important place of learning as this. Bring it in, lads!' The pirates dragged in the bundle and propped it upright.

'Now,' said the Pirate Captain, 'I'm sure you're familiar with my most famous adventure?'

'Is it the one with the slugs?'

'No,' said the Pirate Captain, 'guess again.'

'Ah!' said the Governor, 'it's the adventure where you left your tax return to the last minute!'

'Actually, it was Black Bellamy who had that adventure. I always do mine in April,' said the Pirate Captain. 'One more try.'

The Governor spent a couple of minutes thinking very hard and looking slightly blank.

'*The Monstrous Manatee!*' exclaimed the Pirate Captain, finally losing his patience. 'Everyone knows that. I fought him with my bare hands! It lasted six days! The Monstrous Manatee! I've told you about it at least three times since I arrived here.'

'Of course,' said the Governor, 'the Monstrous Manatee. An excellent adventure. I'd hate to meet that brute in person.'

'Funny you should say that.' The Pirate Captain grinned and whipped the sacking away from the bundle. 'Ta da!'

If you took a loyal but miserable pirate, put his legs in a sleeping bag, tied his arms to his sides as makeshift flippers, dangled seaweed from his head and put some teeth made from orange peel in his mouth, you'd have something that was pretty close to how a monstrous manatee might look. Certainly close enough to fool a landlubbing museum curator, providing you'd told the pirate to stand very still.

The Governor recoiled in fear. 'My goodness, Pirate Captain! Is that him?'

'Certainly is. Stuffed and mounted. Unfortunately he shrank to about a quarter of his size in the process. Note the fearsome claws. He nearly had my eye out with those.'

'Amazing. They look rather like common table forks, but then you did tell me that he was an uncanny and unnatural monster. It really is awfully generous of you, Captain.'

'Oh, it's nothing,' said the Captain modestly. 'The least I could do.'

He looked around the museum and tapped his teeth with his fingernail. 'Now, where to put it? It would be a shame to hide him away, don't you think? What about here, smack bang in the middle of the room? You could put some lanterns on the floor to uplight his face so that he looks extra scary.'

The Governor paced up and down and chewed his lip. 'I'm afraid there's Mister Bonaparte's handkerchief exhibit where you're pointing, Pirate Captain.'

'So there is,' said the Pirate Captain airily. 'I hadn't noticed. Well, that's easily fixed.' He hefted the handkerchief jar over to a dusty corner and casually plonked it down on top of a wastepaper bin.

'There you go,' he said, looking pleased with himself. 'Score one to the Pirate Captain.'

'I beg your pardon?' said the Governor.

'Sorry, forget I said that. I didn't mean to say that bit out loud, I just meant to think it in my head.'

Nine

THE HORROR OF
FANG VALLEY

The next morning the pirate crew were woken up from fitful dreams of hefty ropes and seagulls by a rhythmic banging coming from the garden. They grabbed their dressing gowns or wrapped blankets around their shoulders and traipsed outside to see what was going on, only to find the Pirate Captain, bare-chested against the elements, hammering bits of wood together. He'd obviously been busy. A gigantic beehive towered a full ten feet above the ground. You could tell it was a beehive because right at the top there was a little sign that read in slightly wonky handwriting: 'Welcome, Bees!'

'Hello, lads and Jennifer,' said the Pirate Captain, wiping his brow and putting his hammer down for a moment. He gestured proudly at the creation looming behind him. 'What do you think?'

Most of the pirates didn't know what to think at all, so they just thought about shanties, which was their default thing to think about in situations like this. Taking their lack of response for impressed speechlessness, the Pirate Captain swung open the front of the hive and eagerly

133

waved them forward to have a closer look. Inside, the beehive was divided into a series of lovingly decorated little rooms. There was a dining room, a lounge and even a kitchen. The top of the hive was devoted to a series of offices for the bees to make honey in. The Pirate Captain wasn't sure how much direction bees needed but he had added another sign that said 'PUT HONEY IN HERE' next to a jar with an arrow pointing at it, just to be sure.

'It's brilliant, isn't it?' said the Pirate Captain happily. 'Look, there's the queen's chambers, that's the best bit.[20] I've made a tiny throne for her to look all regal on. And there's a little gym for them to work out in, because it's important my bees remain healthy. And you'll see I've hung up lots of miniature pictures of flowers and pollen and things like that, which bees are into.'

---

20 After mating with his queen a male bee's genitalia will snap off and act as a sort of chastity belt, thus preventing her from mating again with any other males. There's an entire book full of that kind of exciting fact called *How Animals Have Sex* (ISBN 0-297-85112-8), available in most good remainder bookshops/ landfill sites.

'It's certainly not what I was expecting,' said Jennifer.

'Thank you,' said the Captain graciously. 'Once word gets out in the insect community the bees will come flocking. If bees can flock. Between you and me I think I've got a good chance of getting her into the "Readers' Hives" section of next month's *Bee-keeping News*.'

'Where did you get the wood, Captain?' asked the pirate with a scarf, thinking some of the hive looked a little familiar.

'Off the bottom of the pirate boat. She came apart surprisingly easily,' said the Pirate Captain with a shrug. Several of the pirates looked aghast, which they conveyed by putting their hands by their cheeks and making their mouths into an 'O' shape.

'Don't worry, it's not like we'll be needing her any more,' said the Captain reassuringly. He had just picked up his hammer and started banging a few more nails into the wood when he heard a discreet but unmistakably surly cough, and Napoleon's big round head appeared over the top of the garden fence.

'Hello, Pirate Captain,' said Napoleon, in a tone so glacial that it could have had a polar bear standing on top of it.

'Hello, Napoleon,' said the Pirate Captain, equally frosty.

'I hear you have been kind enough to donate to our little museum.'

'Aarrrr, well, one tries to do one's bit.' The Captain stopped banging nails for a moment. 'For the kids really, more than anything.'

'Very public-spirited of you.'

'It's just my way,' said the Captain modestly. He was hoping that might be the end of the conversation, but Napoleon seemed to be lingering. 'Sorry, is there something I can do for you?'

'Yes, Captain, there is.' Napoleon held up a wodge of papers and waggled them under the Captain's nose. 'As you can see, I am trying to write my memoirs.'

'How's that going? Have you got to the part where the Duke of Wellington thumps you yet?'[21]

---

21 Napoleon and the Iron Duke briefly shared a lover, the young actress Mademoiselle George. A bit tactlessly she later announced that Wellington was better in bed.

'No, I have not. In fact I am barely out of the womb – though already I'm showing my preco-ciousness by being the only baby in Corsica who could eat three rusks at a time.'

'Writer's block, eh? Have you tried holding your breath for thirty seconds and wrapping a hot towel around your head? I always find that helps.'

'I do not have writer's block, Captain. I am unable to work because your intolerable banging is making it impossible for me to concentrate.'

'I'm nearly done, so you can keep your hat on. I'm just making my bees a little library. I don't really expect them to read much – it's more of a social thing, somewhere for them to network, pick up other bees, that kind of stuff.'

Napoleon looked up at the towering hive and grimaced. 'What in the name of the revolution *is* this architectural carbuncle?'

'It's not a carbuncle,' said the Captain with a pout. 'It's a beehive.'

'Well, it won't do. It won't do at all,' said Napo-leon. 'Your "beehive" is blocking the light to my garden.'

'I beg your pardon?'

'This,' Napoleon indicated the patch of garden that now lay in the shadow of the hive, 'is where I intend to grow a prize-winning marrow. I have achieved many things in my life, Pirate Captain, and one of the few spheres left for me to conquer is that of outsized vegetable produce. I have no choice but to demand that you dismantle your hive immediately.'

'I will do no such thing,' said the Pirate Captain, drawing himself up to his full height. 'A pirate's beehive is his castle.'

'I'm afraid I must insist.' Napoleon paused and gave a sly smile. 'There are planning regulations to be observed. Not to mention the fact that this construction is clearly an appalling health and safety hazard.'

'Planning regulations?' The Captain snorted and pulled a face. 'Says who?'

Napoleon's sly smile turned into an outright grin. 'Says the new head of the St Helena Residents' Association. I volunteered my services yesterday. You see, Captain, I also like to do my bit for the community.'

And with that, Napoleon flourished his hat triumphantly and ducked back down behind the fence.

The Pirate Captain found the Governor on St Helena's windswept little beach, painting a watercolour of the view out to sea. It was his favourite thing to paint, because all you needed was a ruler and two slightly different shades of grey.

'So I'm sure it's just a bit of a mix-up,' said the Pirate Captain, striding down the shingle towards him, 'but my esteemed neighbour seems to be under the impression that he's the head of the St Helena Residents' Association. You know how these continental types get ideas into their heads. Too much olive oil in their diet, not enough ham, that's the trouble.'

The Governor looked a bit guilty and put down his paint brush. 'Hello again,' he said, with a strained smile. 'Actually Mister Bonaparte is quite correct. He came and offered his services yesterday. The truth is we've never had a St Helena Residents' Association, but he seemed so keen I didn't like to bring that up. Frightfully good of him, really. It's not a problem, is it, Captain?'

The Captain looked at the Governor and thought for a moment. He prided himself on his ability to multitask, both looking and thinking at the same time. Sometimes he even combined it with walking and eating.

'Not a problem as such, Governor,' he said eventually, 'But the thing is, do you remember how you told me that St Helena is "a little piece of England"?'

'Oh yes,' said the Governor brightly. 'And then you got rather confused and asked how on earth they had managed to lop off a piece of England and tow it thousands of miles away into the middle of the Atlantic. And then I explained that I was talking figuratively, but you didn't really seem to grasp that and went on speculating that they must have used porpoises attached to ropes. It ended up being quite a long conversation, as I recall.'

'Yes, well, aside from how it got here, my point is this: St Helena is a little piece of England. And what is England famous for?'

The Governor shrugged. 'Our delicate cuisine? Our fine dentition? Our uninhibited raw sexuality?'

'Democracy!' exclaimed the Pirate Captain. 'England is famous for inventing democracy.'

'Are you sure that wasn't the Greeks?'

'No, it was the English, same as everything else. Now don't get me wrong, I'm certain Napoleon would do a great job as head of the residents' association. But it's just not very *democratic*, simply appointing him like that, is it? Can't imagine Queen Victoria would approve.'

'Oh dear, I suppose not.' The Governor shook his bushy mutton chops anxiously. 'What do you suggest I do?'

'Well, I'm no expert on these matters, Governor, but I think you have to call an election.'

'An election?' The Governor paced back and forth and pondered for a moment. 'But who on earth would stand against Mister Bonaparte? I mean to say, he's incredibly overqualified for the position as it is.'

'Aaarrrr.' The Pirate Captain frowned. 'That's true. It would have to be someone with proven organisational abilities, because I suspect running a residents' association involves a great deal of hard work, much like running a pirate boat. They'd need to be well travelled, a man of the world. And it would have to be someone the electorate could trust, so, really, you'd want them to have a pleasant, open face.'

'Pirate Captain!' exclaimed the Governor. '*You* have a pleasant, open face!'

The Pirate Captain pretended to blush, which is quite a tricky thing to pull off. 'Me? But I'm just a humble bee-keeper. Happy in my quiet life, rearing honey. Not the kind of fellow who lusts after political power at all.'

'But, Captain,' said the Governor, a pleading look in his eyes. 'You wouldn't be doing it for you. You'd be doing it for the good of democracy. For England!'

'Oh well, when you put it like that, I suppose

it's hard to refuse.' The Pirate Captain hunted around in his pockets for a second and then pulled out something small and shiny with VOTE PIRATE CAPTAIN FOR HEAD OF THE ST HELENA RESIDENTS' ASSOCIATION written across it. 'Here you go, Governor, have a badge.'

Ten

PERIL IN CRAB CITY

Letters published in the *St Helena Gazette*, 1815.

Dear *St Helena Gazette* Letters page,

I'm sure I'm not the only resident to find our new arrival, the Pirate Captain, a real breath of fresh air. I especially enjoy his stentorian nose, and I think I probably speak for all of us when I say that he has the most luxuriant beard ever. I wonder how he gets it so silky-looking? Perhaps, if he is not too busy, he could pen an article on the subject for our little gazette. I also like his shoes.

Hugs,

An Anonymous Islander

Dear Sirs,

I am just writing to congratulate our island's Amateur Dramatics Society on last Thursday's fine staging of *The Tempest*. I think Monsieur Bonaparte deserves special praise for his brilliant and commanding Ferdinand – such a shame that the whole performance was somewhat let down by the rather hammy overacting of the Pirate Captain's Miranda. Otherwise, four stars!

Salutations distinguées,

A long-time devoted reader

Dear *St Helena Gazette* Letters page,

What a pity that our island's recent garden fête, which was for the most part a fun day out for all, suffered from such erratic judging in the Heaviest Marrow section of the competition. How Napoleon's frankly anaemic-looking entry was judged to have been superior to the Pirate Captain's gargantuan legume I will never know.

Hugs,

An Anonymous Islander

Dear Sirs,

I was recently unfortunate enough to purchase a jar of the Pirate Captain's 'Famous Nautical Honey'. Perhaps in piratical circles it is usual for honey to consist mostly of bee heads, soil and seawater, but I would not recommend it to anyone of more refined tastes. By the way, I hear that Monsieur Bonaparte will be signing copies of his memoirs, *A Long Road To Greatness*, at the local bookshop this coming Saturday. Make sure you get there early or risk disappointment!

Salutations distinguées,

A long-time devoted reader

Dear *Hot and Nautical* Magazine,

Last week something amazing happened that I thought your readers might be interested in. I was at home in my cabin, minding my own business, when I heard a knock at the door. Well, I wasn't expecting anybody, so imagine my surprise when I opened it to find a stunning redhead standing in the hallway, wearing only a daring negligee! She had curves in all the right places and legs that just wouldn't quit! [letter continues page 2]

Dear *St Helena Gazette* Letters page,

Sorry, best forget all that. Bit of a mix-up with the envelopes there. What I had intended to bring to the attention of your readers was not an unlikely erotic encounter with a flame-haired temptress, but rather the fact that this Friday the Pirate Captain will be signing copies of his memoirs, *Fine Hams I Have Known*, at the local butcher's.

Hugs,

An Anonymous Islander

Dear Sirs,

Thank you for a fascinating article on the wild-life of the English countryside. It was an enthralling account of the kinds of creature we could meet here on St Helena, if it was a completely different place. Most interesting was the passage on the cuckoo and the impertinent way it muscles into another bird's nest and grows fat on worms intended for others.

One individual who seems to have learned a great deal from the cuckoo is a certain Pirate

Captain. I saw him at his recent book signing, oiling his way into the affections of the islanders by wearing a ridiculously ostentatious pair of voluminous trousers. As I watched from behind a goat carcass, it occurred to me that they looked a lot like the curtains that were recently stolen from Monsieur Bonaparte's washing line. A coincidence? Perhaps not.

Salutations distinguées,

A long-time devoted reader

Dear *St Helena Gazette* Letters Page,

In your last issue you published a letter that implied our island's most colourful character, the Pirate Captain, was not entirely honest. As an impartial observer, I would like to point out that he is renowned for his sense of fair play, as demonstrated by the recent cricket match on the green.

One particular incident springs to mind, when the Pirate Captain had knocked up a masterful forty-five runs. You may recall that in the first ball of a new over, he hit a magnificent shot towards the pavilion, where Monsieur Napoleon was supposed to be fielding. Not only did the Frenchman attempt to field the ball when it was clearly over the boundary, but he also caught it in his hat. In a demonstration of good-natured sportsmanship, the Pirate Captain only disputed his dismissal for two hours with Monsieur Napoleon and the umpire (who clearly had the sun in his eyes at the time), before conceding. But there was no way he was out, no matter what that little megalomaniac might say.

Hugs,

An Anonymous Islander

Dear Sirs,

I notice your 'Anonymous Islander' makes no mention of the Pirate Captain's illegal use of cannons in the cricket match. I wonder if he'll use similar tactics at next week's public debate? I wouldn't put it past him.

On a lighter note, I would like to add how marvellous Monsieur Bonaparte was looking yesterday, walking up and down in his brand-new spats. Anyone with half a brain would realise that he's the natural choice for Head of the Residents' Association. You can't trust men with beards, can you? They're clearly trying to hide something.

Salutations distinguées,

A long-time devoted reader

PS As a keen student of anatomy I would just like to say please please please please please can we have more of Jean the 'bathing beauty'?

Eleven

SUBSTATION ALPHA
MUST BE DESTROYED!

The pirates walked briskly back and forth across the living room, which now, according to the banner hung across the wall, wasn't called the living room, it was called the 'Election Campaign Headquarters'. The walking briskly back and forth didn't achieve much but the Pirate Captain liked how it made everything look busy and dynamic. So far, most of the morning's strategy meeting had been devoted to coming up with a political logo. The pirates were very keen that it should reflect both the Captain's caring, inclusive side, but also his tough leadership qualities. After a lot of debate they had eventually decided on a picture of a bush baby holding a brick.

'So, what's next on the agenda, chief of staff?' asked the Pirate Captain, plumping himself down on the sofa.

'We should probably work on your manifesto, Captain,' replied the chief of staff, who was formerly known as the pirate with a scarf.

'That sounds exciting. Manifesto. Man-i-fes-to . . . Any ideas?'

'Well,' said the pirate in green, consulting his clipboard. 'I thought we'd emphasise your commitment to free healthcare for all.'

'Oh yes. It's like I'm always saying – if I decide I want an extra ear, or a double set of teeth, like a shark, I should be able to get it paid for by the state. Here's the slogan: "The Pirate Captain Says: Extra appendages from cradle to grave." Write that down.'

'I don't think that's in the remit of the Head of the Residents' Association, Captain,' said the pirate in red, who had been put on duty making bunting to keep him out of trouble. The Pirate Captain threw an election pamphlet at his head.

'Pirate Captain, has it occurred to you that perhaps you're not really cut out for politics?' said Jennifer, who was allowed to speak freely about this sort of thing, because the rest of the pirates assumed that as a girl she wasn't attuned to social niceties. 'Politics is about belief and ideology. Whereas you just don't seem to have anything approaching a consistent opinion. Half an hour ago you were saying crime was caused by poverty. Then five minutes later you said it was caused by pirates who didn't bring you a cup of tea when you fancied one. And now you think . . .'

'That crime is caused by uncomfortable sofas and crumbs in your beard,' said the Pirate Captain with absolute certainty.

'See?' said Jennifer.

The Pirate Captain leaped off the sofa. 'Ah, but that's my hidden strength,' he said with a cheerful wink. 'I don't have any actual views on anything so I'll just give the electorate exactly what they want! It's a golden opportunity to skip that whole idealistic young candidate stuff and jump straight to the part where I sell out to powerful lobby groups.'

'I'm afraid St Helena doesn't really have powerful lobby groups, unless you count the tramp who quite likes the earwigs,' said the pirate with a scarf. 'But we do have some polling data on the kind of things the islanders like.'

He handed the Captain a list. It read:

Things that the islanders like:
Being left alone
Queen Victoria
Nice weather
Crisps
Pictures of cute animals
Politeness

'Right,' said the Captain, after a bit of deliberation. 'They like Queen Victoria. They like crisps. Bingo! We'll make a statue of Queen Victoria out of crisps, thus killing two birds with one stone. Honestly, a political mind like mine only comes along once in a generation.'

Before the Pirate Captain could get any further with his crisp/statue plans, they were interrupted by a sharp tap at the window. There, pressed against the glass was the small grimy face of an island urchin.

'In 1807,' the urchin began to intone seriously, 'Napoleon defeated Russian forces at the battle of Friedland. And in 1807 the Pirate Captain got his arm stuck in a drain for an entire month, after trying to pick up what he thought was a shilling, but which turned out to be a shiny pebble. In 1808 Napoleon captured the city of Madrid. And in 1808 the Pirate Captain's ill-advised attempt at home-brewing grog burnt down half of Portsmouth. In 1809 Napoleon successfully annexed the Papal States. And in 1809 the Pirate Captain tried to start a short-lived business painting horses to look like zebras. Who would you trust with your children's future? This advertisement was brought to you by the Committee to Re-elect Napoleon.'

And with that the urchin scampered off in the direction of another house.

'That's a bit cheeky,' exclaimed the Pirate Captain.

'I certainly didn't expect Napoleon to go negative at this stage of the campaign,' nodded the pirate with a scarf. 'There's only one thing for it, Captain.'

'You think we should spend some more time discussing my logo? That's the bit I've enjoyed most so far.'

'No, Captain. I think you need to get out there and set the record straight. Meet your public. And, most importantly, kiss some babies.'

The Pirate Captain sat back down and furrowed

his brow. 'Aaarrr. Not really sure about the baby-kissing business. Always found babies have a bit of a funny smell about them. And I don't want one sicking up all over my nice blousy shirt, which I believe they're prone to do at the drop of a hat.'

'Baby-kissing is a tried and tested way of getting votes, Captain.'

The Captain didn't look convinced. 'Thing is, number two, what's the voting age nowadays?'

'It's eighteen, sir.'

'Exactly!' The Pirate Captain waggled an informative finger. 'So there's not much point lavishing all this attention on babies when they can't even vote for me, is there? I should be concentrating on the eighteen-year-olds. And you know which other bit of the electorate is often unfairly overlooked? Women. So really it makes a lot more sense for me to spend the morning kissing eighteen-year-old women.'[22]

---

22   Liechtenstein women got the vote in 1984, which is a full two years after *Tron* came out.

'Right, here we go, number two,' said the Pirate Captain, hopping up onto a treasure chest that the pirates had set out in the middle of the village green as a makeshift soapbox. The pirate with a scarf handed him a megaphone made out of an empty milk bottle.

'Oh, this is good,' said the Captain, waggling the milk bottle. 'I like the way it makes my voice go all booming.' He held it up to his lips, and then put it down again, because he realised he hadn't decided what to say. 'What do you suggest I start off with?' he asked the pirate with a scarf.

'You're strong on immigration, Captain.'

'Yes, good idea.' The Captain cleared his throat and spoke into the megaphone, waving at the small crowd of islanders who had mostly turned up to see what all the noise was about. 'Hello there, people of St Helena! Did you know that there has recently been a huge increase in immigration? This is a small island, and it cannot be expected to cope with an influx of foreigners stealing our jobs and our earwigs. Only last month a band of actual *pirates* was allowed to stay on the island. Are these the kind of people we want as neighbours?'

But before the Pirate Captain really had a chance to get going, he noticed the same urchin from before was whispering something to one of the watching islanders. Soon there was a murmuring amongst the crowd and they all started to drift off down towards the beach.

'Excuse me!' said the Pirate Captain, calling after them. 'I haven't got to the bit where I tell you my bold plans to hollow out the island and put some kind of steam engine in there. That way we could follow the international dateline around the globe and none of us would ever get any older. A vote for the Pirate Captain is a vote for eternal life!'

'They've gone, Captain,' said Jennifer.

'I think something is afoot,' said the pirate in green.

The Pirate Captain sighed. 'Well then, I suppose we'd better go and see what on earth could be more interesting than me.'

All the islanders were standing in a circle, looking at something on the shingle in front of them. Snatches of excited chatter drifted up from the beach, and the pirates hurried forward to see what all the fuss was about. When they finally got to the ring of islanders they saw, lying there in an awkward heap, a gigantic dead squid splayed across the rocks. It was about ten feet long, with one big yellow eye the size of a plate, and a body that was the sort of greyish colour that the Pirate Captain tended to turn when he'd eaten too many sausages in one sitting.

'Is that it?' said the Pirate Captain, who couldn't help but look unimpressed. 'I was expecting something a bit more exciting than a big washed-up squid. Still, it will make a nice change for dinner, I suppose.'

'How can you even suggest such a thing?' said an appalled lady islander. 'To treat her like this, even now she's dead!'

'I beg your pardon?' said the Captain, baffled.

'There appears to be more to this matter than a simple beaching,' explained the Governor.

'Really? You suspect foul play?'

'Moider!' said the pirate from the Bronx, who pretty much lived for these moments.

'Not murder,' said the Governor gravely. 'Suicide.'

'What on earth makes you think that?' asked Jennifer. 'Squids and whales and things wash up all the time, don't they?'

'They do, young lady,' said Napoleon, who seemed to be looking very pleased with himself. 'But this poor creature was found with a *note* in its beak.'

'A note? Really?' said the Pirate Captain, incredulous. 'There you go. I always thought they had brains the size of beads.'

'I must say, Captain, it doesn't look good,' said the Governor, handing over a soggy piece of paper and shooting him a disappointed frown. The Pirate Captain fished out his spectacles and started to read:

To whom it may concern,

I cannot go on any longer. I know people think us giant squid are just unfathomable monsters of the

166

deep, but we have feelings too. And it is time the
world learnt the terrible truth. For several years now
the Pirate Captain and I have been carrying on an
illicit affair. Many times I have asked the Pirate
Captain to do right by me, but he refuses, always tell-
ing me that he cannot be seen having a relationship
with a giant squid because of the harm it would do to
his public image. Also, sometimes he hits me.
Anyhow, just yesterday I discovered I was pregnant
with the Pirate Captain's secret love child! I told the
Pirate Captain about this and he flew into a rage and
said he would never help support his half-squid/half-
pirate progeny and then he hit me some more. So
now I am going to commit suicide by beaching myself.

Goodbye, cruel world
The Giant Squid

The Pirate Captain looked up from the note and
a row of accusatory faces looked back at him.

'Well, that's absurd on so many levels I barely
know where to begin,' he protested. 'For a start,
where would a Giant Squid get St Helena Residents' Association notepaper? Also the

handwriting is normal-sized, whereas surely it should be giant-sized. And finally, just look at the thing! It's hideous. If I *was* to date a squid, which I'm not saying I would, though you should never rule these things out, especially if you've been at sea for a few months, but if I was, I'd go for one of the more attractive species, like *Sepioteuthis sepioidea*, the Caribbean Reef Squid. Or one of those iridescent ones, they're actually very pretty. Certainly not this flabby, beaked monstrosity, anyhow.'

But despite the Captain's protestations several of the islanders and even a couple of the more easily swayed pirates were already trudging away, muttering things under their breath.

'Now, look here,' said the Pirate Captain, waving uselessly after them. 'I wouldn't have a clue how to begin to impregnate a giant squid. My zoological knowledge is famously ropy.' His words floated away with the crowds across the beach.

'What unfortunate timing,' said Napoleon, giving the Pirate Captain a consoling squeeze on his bicep. 'And I was really hoping this election would be settled on the issues, rather than what are frankly irrelevant character flaws. But you know what the public's appetite for scandal is like.' He doffed his hat and skipped off down the beach. 'Anyhow, good luck at tomorrow's debate, Captain,' he called over his shoulder. 'May the best man win.'

'It's character assassination!' exclaimed the Pirate Captain, back at his Campaign HQ. He angrily flung a rosette across the room and knocked one of his flying ducks off the wall in the process. 'It's a sad day for democracy when this kind of thing replaces mature debate on what really matters, like who has the best hair and other things like that.'

'The opinion polls certainly don't look good, Captain,' said the pirate with a scarf, studying a chart.

'Is there any way you could sugar-coat it for me?' asked the Captain. 'You know I'm not very good at dealing with things I don't want to hear.'

'Well, the good news is that when asked "do you think the Pirate Captain has nice eyes?" you score very highly, right across all demographic groups. And the response is also overwhelmingly positive that "Yes, the Pirate Captain does have a certain indefinable élan." But I'm afraid Napoleon is ahead of you when it comes to "the person we would most trust when left alone with our teenage daughters". And of the population's two lunatics I'm afraid both think they're Napoleon rather than you.'

'That's a blow,' said the Captain, rubbing his chin. 'I'm normally very popular amongst the lunatic constituency.'

'And unfortunately with the debate tomorrow, there's not much time for this squid scandal to blow over.' The pirates all looked at their shoes in a bit of a funk.

'You can't just let him get away with it!' exploded Jennifer. 'I know we're bee-keepers now and we're all about quiet reflection and solitude and all that rot, but that doesn't mean we have to lose all our vim and pep.'

'I still have plenty of pep,' said the Pirate Captain defensively. 'I'm just not going to stoop to that cove's devious level. We're going to take a different, more direct approach.'

'Are we going to run him through?' asked the pirate in green hopefully.

'Let's feed him to the sharks!' said the pirate with gout. He bit his cutlass to look extra fearsome.

'Slice his gizzard!' said the albino pirate.

'I'd like to see the colour of his innards!' said the pirate who liked kittens and sunsets.

There was quite a lot of excited roaring, and the suggestions for revenge on Napoleon became more robust and bloodthirsty.

'Better than that, lads,' said the Pirate Captain. 'Get the dressing-up box.'

Twelve

CREATURE PARADE!

Napoleon's bedroom was tastefully decorated with lots of paintings of the great man himself. There was one of him standing on a pile of dead Spaniards with two women in chain-mail bikinis clinging adoringly on to his shoulders. Another showed him standing on top of a pile of dead Russians with two women in fur bikinis and Cossack hats clinging adoringly on to his legs. The paintings went on in pretty much this same vein right around the room. But at the moment it was difficult to appreciate the artwork, because it was night and the lights were out. Everything was still and silent, except for Napoleon's snores and a faint scratching sound from outside. Gradually, the window inched open and a host of shadowy figures crept inside the room.

'Shh . . .' said the shadowy figure with the stentorian nose.[23] 'Don't make a sound until everyone is in position.'

---

23 Legend has it that the Sphinx lost its nose when Napoleon's artillery shot it off during target practice. In fact, sketches from the early eighteenth century show a noseless Sphinx, suggesting that it was lost long before Napoleon's expedition in 1798. It is far more likely that it was knocked off by Obelix, as depicted in *Asterix and Cleopatra* (Goscinny & Uderzo, 1965).

The last two shadowy figures closed the window behind them and opened the curtains to let the moonlight in, while a third tiptoed over to Napoleon. He placed a pale hand on his shoulder and shook it gently. Napoleon opened his left eye.

'Why,' said Napoleon, 'is there an ant with a scarf standing over my bed? Is this a new trend for burglars? Dressing as anthropomorphic insects?'

The ant with a scarf composed himself. 'You are dreaming, Napoleon. I am an ant with a scarf who walks like a man, which is so surreal that it could only be part of a dream.' He paused and waggled his abdomen. 'Now, hold my ant hand and I will take you on an amazing fantasy ride that will astound you and also provide useful advice on your waking life. Come!' The ant with a scarf took Napoleon's hand, and made some whooshing noises to imply movement.

'Where are you taking me? Are we going to fly through the sky or something?' asked Napoleon.

'Um, no,' said the ant with a scarf. 'This dream will happen entirely in your bedroom.'

The Pirate Captain had once told the crew that if you ever found yourself having a two-way conversation with a piece of furniture or dancing a waltz with a man made out of spaghetti, then the chances were it was a dream, because that sort of thing very rarely happens in real life.[24] The way to be *really* certain that you were dreaming was to look out for food that you had eaten the previous evening playing an active part in what was going on. Sure enough, in this dream there followed a sequence of bizarre imagery, no doubt loaded with symbolism and the kind of food one would expect a Frenchman to eat before bed, especially if you had been through his bins earlier that evening. Half a dozen hens chased some croissants around the room, a baguette did a little dance, and then a couple of snails waved their eye stalks around and sang a song about guts without much enthusiasm.

---

24   The lack of logic in dreams is probably linked to the reduced flow of information between the hippocampus and the neocortex during REM states.

'Tell me, ant, does this dream go anywhere?' said Napoleon. 'It seems a little directionless.'

'It's definitely dreamlike though?' said the ant with a scarf.

'Oh yes. Very confusing and unlikely,' said Napoleon.

'Good. Now, Napoleon, you shall encounter the first of three famous generals. They're all *very* keen to meet you and want to pass on some valuable advice. So, without any further ado, he's come all the way from Ancient Greece, he conquered most of the known world and he died from drinking too much ... let's have a big hand for *Alexander the Great!*'

A small troop of Greek soldiers shuffled out of Napoleon's wardrobe and had lots of fun bashing their swords together and banging shields in a pretend fight. In their enthusiasm, they may have used more nautical expressions than you would expect from a bunch of Greek hoplites, but the effect was certainly dramatic. Eventually the soldiers parted to reveal Alexander the Great who, presumably because of twisted dream logic, looked a lot like a Victorian lady dragged up as a man, complete with toga, helmet and a pencil-thin moustache that later generations would identify with David Niven.

'Hail, Napoleon!' said Alexander the Great in a voice rather higher than Napoleon expected. 'I am Alexander the Great, scourge of the Persians. For my whole life I fought many battles, conquering all before me and riding my horse about.'

'Bucephalus,' said Napoleon.

'I beg your pardon?' said Alexander the Great.

'Bucephalus – your horse. That was his name.'

'Was it?' said Alexander the Great. He slapped his thigh and gave Napoleon a dazzling grin. 'How exciting! It must have been great to ride about across the world and conquer things. But yes, Napoleon, I remember now, and he was a lovely horse, very keen on sugar lumps.'

Alexander the Great strode back and forth across the room while a couple of Greek soldiers unfurled a map of the Ancient World. 'Observe, Napoleon – the world of my day. Do you recall the siege of Termessos?'

Napoleon sat up in bed. 'I do! It's one of my favourite battles! It was a masterpiece of strategy, because even though you lost, you understood the . . .'

'Excuse me, it's my story,' interrupted Alexander the Great. 'Yes, I marched my armies to the city and surrounded it. We besieged its walls, but soon I realised that Termessos was impregnable. There was no way I could win and if it had been a *man* rather than a *city*, it would have been the *better man* in this instance. So I effectively surrendered to the better man.'

'You *could* put it like that,' said Napoleon doubtfully.

'I do,' said Alexander, 'and by conceding this battle, I went on to win many more and got my name in all the history books, so ultimately it was a good thing. If I had wasted my time on fighting a hopeless lost cause I might not be here to tell you this today. Heed these words! And on that note, here's your second visitor from the past.'

Alexander opened the wardrobe and waved another figure forward. This general was preceded by a small crowd of scruffy-looking men whooping and riding brooms as if they were horses.

'Make way, my Mongol hordes! Make way for your captain, the terrible Genghis Khan!' Genghis Khan rode through the Mongols on his broom, knocked over a vase and did a little pantomime where he pretended his horse was out of control. For some reason, Genghis Khan wore a ten-gallon hat and had a long thin moustache sprouting from on top of another moustache. He also had a magnificent beard and a pleasant, open face which looked quite sleepy, as if Genghis Khan would normally be in bed at this time of night.

'Yee ha!' said Genghis Khan. He threw his cowboy hat into the air and shot it with a pistol. 'Howdy, pardner. I'm Genghis Khan. Way back in the olden days, I pillaged my way across Asia, Europe and I think India as well. My horsemen rode across the prairies, causing trouble and making mayhem.'

'Of course, Genghis,' said Napoleon. 'I know all about it. I've spent years studying your campaigns. You were my specialist subject at General Academy.'

'Then you will know my greatest mistake, Napoleon Bonaparte. The mistake that cost me my life and my reputation, leaving me as nothing more than an academic footnote of interest only to boring history students who don't get invited to parties. Yes, if I could live my life again I would be a good deal less stubborn. I never retreated and that, alas, was my downfall.'

'Never retreated? Yes, you did, Genghis. That was the whole point of being a Mongol, you'd attack people and then dash off on horses, then come back and fight a bit more and then ride off again. You *invented* that kind of fighting.'

Genghis Khan played with the ends of his moustache and thought for a moment. 'Is that what they're telling you in the future? Aarrr. That'll be because history is written by the victor, whereas I was the loser on account of my inability to retreat. And look at me now, you scurvy knave – I'm dead! Remember this. Remember. REMEMBER!'

With that, Genghis Khan galloped back into the wardrobe. Napoleon yawned, and glanced at his bedside clock. 'Who's the third general, ant with a scarf? Ideally I'd like to meet Boudicca or Sun Tzu. Is that possible?'

'Better than that,' said the ant with a scarf. 'You are about to meet a general of warfare yet to come. Say hello to General 2893B, from the year *1988*!'

This time the wardrobe opened and a regimented unit of black-clad figures marched in robotic unison towards the bed, humming a sinister dirge.[25] At their head stood an awkward figure with a hook for a hand and tin foil on his face.

'Hello, General 2893B,' said Napoleon, waving. 'I don't know anything about you, but I have a suspicion as to what you're going to tell me.'

General 2893B looked down at a piece of paper and spoke in a deep monotone. 'People of Earth, I

---

25 The best sinister futuristic dirges were made by Daphne Oram and Delia Derbyshire at the BBC's Radiophonic Workshop. If you prefer something a bit more melodic try Paddy Kingsland instead.

am General 2893B of the future. With my mindless legions I have fought throughout the solar system, on the surface of the moon against monsters, in the gas mines of Jupiter against robots and on the ice fields of Mercury against the Irish. I am undefeated because I have complete knowledge of all the greatest generals in history.'

'And what do they say about me in 1988?' asked Napoleon.

'I had never heard of you until I was asked to appear in your dream, when I thought it was only polite to look you up. It turns out that in my time Napoleon is known for only one thing – being beaten in an election for Head of the Residents' Association on St Helena. He lost to the greatest man we know of, the legendary Pirate Captain. You are almost forgotten, simply because your foolish pride prevented you from letting the Pirate Captain win uncontested. It's a crying shame.'

General 2893B bowed, whispered, 'Was that all right?' to somebody behind him, and then squashed back inside the wardrobe with the other bits of dream.

'So, Napoleon, to sum up, what have we learnt from tonight?' said the ant with a scarf. 'We have seen generals from the past and future and all three have illustrated the advantages of caving in to your opposition. I hope that's pretty clear.'

'Oh, dream spirit, you have shown me such wondrous things,' said Napoleon, 'and it's a bit much for me to take in right now. I'll certainly bear in mind everything I have seen and I wouldn't want you to think you've wasted your time. But this dream has made me strangely tired, which is odd given that I'm supposedly fast asleep.'

'We will now depart for mysterious realms,' said the ant with a scarf, 'but it really is incredibly important to pay attention to these prophetic dreams. Ignore them at your peril.' He drew the curtains and waited until Napoleon's snores resumed. The generals clambered back out of the cupboard.

'He's off,' whispered Alexander the Great. 'Let's get out of here before he wakes up and ruins the whole thing.'

'Absolutely,' said Genghis Khan, 'just as soon as we've all had a chance to go through his drawers and try on his medals.'

Thirteen

CRASHING ZEPPELINS FOR A LIVING

The Pirate Captain and Napoleon stood behind a curtain at the village hall, each trying to look more relaxed than the other. Napoleon did this mainly by ostentatiously yawning, whilst the Captain pretended to be busy concentrating on the newspaper crossword.

'So,' said the Captain, in as blasé a voice as he could do. 'Had any interesting dreams lately?'

Napoleon stopped yawning and nodded. 'Do you know, as a matter of fact, Captain, I have. I dreamed that a rather overweight cowboy man was trying to persuade me to do something, though for the life of me I couldn't work out what it was.'

'Really? No clue at all?' said the Captain, a little crestfallen. 'Because I knew a fellow once who ignored his dreams and he ended up cursed. Smelt like asparagus from that day on. Couldn't do a thing about it. So best to take them seriously.'

'The strange thing is,' said Napoleon, 'my dreams are usually very realistic. Whereas this one was like something an idiot child might have staged.'

'Still. Those idiot children *know* things, don't they? I generally do whatever they tell me.'

The Pirate Captain was about to go into more detail about the many things he had done at the behest of idiot children, but at that moment the curtain came up and the Governor called them forward onto the stage. The pirate crew were all loyally sitting in the front rows and a handful of St Helena residents were lounging at the back. A goat wandered around the hall eating the chairs. There was a ripple of polite applause as the candidates took their places behind two lecterns. Napoleon saluted the audience, whilst the Pirate Captain waved with both hands and stuck his fingers in his mouth and whistled.

The Governor motioned for quiet and sat down at a desk in the middle of the stage with a little stack of cards in front of him. Each card had a question on it which he had carefully copied out of an old copy of Hansard the night before, because despite repeated requests, the islanders hadn't submitted any questions at all and the pirates seemed to have missed the point of the debate entirely and focused on queries that were either rhetorical ('What's up, candidates?') or irrelevant ('Who is Britain's heaviest farmer?'). The Governor shuffled the cards and everyone held their breath:

- Napoleon held his breath because this was a tense moment.
- The Governor held his breath because he didn't want to accidentally blow the questions all over the floor after spending so much time getting them neatly stacked.
- The Pirate Captain held his breath because he was trying to use his 'powers' to force a question about beard maintenance to mystically rise from the pack.
- The pirates held their breath because of the 'elephant in the room'. There wasn't an actual elephant in the Village Hall today, but if there had been, knocking over stacks of leaflets and drinking the Pirate Captain's tea, it would have had 'Pirate of the Year Awards Debacle' painted on its flanks. Holding their breath wouldn't make the Pirate

Captain any better at answering questions, but the pirates wanted to fit in.

- The goat didn't hold its breath.

The Governor cleared his throat and picked up a card. 'Candidates, here is your first question: as Head of the Residents' Association, how do you plan to boost St Helena's image overseas and increase our popularity as a tourist destination? Monsieur Bonaparte? Would you like to kick us off?'[26]

'A fine question,' said Napoleon, thumping his lectern dramatically. 'We need to play up what this island is already famous for. So I intend to construct a theme park called Napoleon Land. The centrepiece will be a rollercoaster shaped like my hat, which will not only be a physical rollercoaster, but also an emotional one

---

26 Although a large majority of people who watched the Kennedy/Nixon presidential debate on television thought that Kennedy performed best, those listening to it on radio rated the candidates about equal. Which suggests that for most of the electorate 'not sweating like a pig' is a key political consideration.

as it will reflect the ups and downs of my cele-brated life to date. And you will be able to buy "Napoleon-floss", though this will just be garlic-flavoured candyfloss.'

Everybody clapped, and the Governor turned to the Pirate Captain, who tugged thoughtfully at his lapels. 'My esteemed opponent makes an interest-ing case,' he said, 'but what you have to remember about tourists is that when they're visiting an exotic island like ours they expect a bit of anthropological colour. So to this end I have bold plans for every St Helenite to wear those great big plate things in their lower lips. And maybe get some of those brass rings that make your necks go all long and floppy, like the hill tribes have. Finally, I'm all for stealing one of the big heads from Easter Island, if that's what it takes.'

The audience applauded again and a few of the pirates did their best impressions of Easter Island statues. The pirate with a scarf stopped chewing the tip of his scarf quite so nervously and breathed a sigh of relief, because the Captain seemed to be handling the situation much better than he had expected.

The Governor picked up another question. 'St Helena has a reasonably stable housing market. However, if circumstances were to change, what fiscal measures would the candidates take to restore equilibrium? Mister Bonaparte?'

'Well, Governor, as a man who follows the property market with great enthusiasm . . .'

As Napoleon began to drone on, the Pirate Captain realised he was in a bit of a fix. The problem was that several of his crew had recently hit that age where all they ever wanted to talk about over feasts was either having babies or getting mortgages. Eventually the Pirate Captain had found himself so busy having to run through pirates who started on these topics of conversation that he had banned any mention of them from the boat. And as a result he didn't know the first thing about housing markets.

Fortunately, the pirate with a scarf had thought ahead. The Pirate Captain felt around in his pocket for the piece of paper that his loyal deputy had pressed into his hand that morning. 'Please read this before the debate, Pirate

Captain,' he had said, 'it will help you deal with any question thrown at you.' The Captain really *had* intended to read it beforehand, but he hadn't quite got round to it, because instead he'd ended up playing a game with the crew that involved seeing who could fit the most marshmallows in their mouth and still say 'big barnacles'. He had managed eighteen. So now, as surreptitiously as he could, he slipped on his reading glasses and unfolded the note.

'DEBATE BRIEFING – HOW TO WIN'

---

1. SMILE AND MAKE EYE CONTACT: Statistics show that floating voters are 45 per cent more likely to vote for the candidate who looks happiest.
2. KEEP YOUR MOUTH MOIST: If it's dry, suck a peppermint – there's a bag in your left pocket.
3. CONCENTRATE: Focus on the debate. Really, Pirate Captain, please don't let your mind wander. I can't state this strongly enough.

Good luck! The lads are rooting for you.

The Captain was pleased to see that Jennifer had also kissed the bottom of the paper and left a lip print.

With Napoleon still in full flow, the pirate Captain decided to tackle the list in order. First of all he did his most winning grin, opened his eyes really wide and swept his gaze across the whole audience, taking care to make lingering eye contact with every single person there. Several of the islanders flinched, two or three looked petrified and one old man fled the room. Sure enough, after his smiling teeth had been exposed for a full five minutes, his mouth was feeling quite dry, so he fished around in his pocket for the bag of peppermints and popped one into his mouth. Then he began to concentrate. This wasn't really something the Pirate Captain had much experience of, but he'd seen other people concentrate, and he knew that it involved furrowing your brow and pursing your lips. So he furrowed his brow and pursed his lips, and was happy to find that concentrating was a lot easier than he had been expecting. In fact, the Captain was so pleased with how well his concentrating was going that he decided to treat himself to another peppermint.

Years of circumnavigating the globe had eventually persuaded the Pirate Captain that the world might be spherical after all, much like a peppermint. And as he held it between finger and thumb, a strange thought struck him – *what if this mint was a world itself?* What sort of world would it be? Probably the green stripes would be the habitable continents, covered with fields and tiny sugary forests, while the white stripes would be frozen wastelands, perhaps inhabited by savage creatures that looked like a cross between a polar bear and a centipede and fired electricity from their antlers. The natives of Mintworld would live in cities lining the frontier between the wasteland and the habitable green stripes, with the streets covered with statues of their god, who would have a luxuriant beard and a pleasant, open face. Looking closer at the peppermint, the Pirate Captain felt he could almost see one of the biggest cities on Mintworld, a bustling hive of rogues and adventurers who hunted the polar-bear-centipede things in the wasteland for their fur and meat. Many crews would sail from the city in great mintships, which were captained by brave characters much admired by the citizens. A particularly dashing mintshipman was known for his daring and clean good looks. Female Mintworlders probably had posters of him on their walls and sighed when they thought about his broad neck and strong arms. But the mintshipman only had eyes for one Mintworld lady and that was a lovely princess who lived in a big tower on the other side of the wasteland, where her cruel father had imprisoned her for some mean reason that the Pirate Captain couldn't think of right now, but it was probably something to do with a prophecy. The mintshipman would sail across the wasteland for many days, avoiding perils like mysterious gas, robots and potholes, all to spend some time gazing at the lovely princess, who had a nice singing voice and wore one of those flimsy frocks that go a bit see-through in the right light. After he'd done a spot of gazing, he'd get bored and sail off for a while, but a couple of weeks later he'd be back to moon around and look all romantic.

At some point, decided the Pirate Captain, the mintshipman would get sick of mucking about and he'd pluck up the courage to go and talk to the princess's father, the King. He'd have a big row with him and they'd use all kinds of insults, including swearing, like calling each other —, — and ——. Eventually, the King would decree that the mintshipman could meet his daughter only if he could make a gigantic fry-up to feed the whole of his nasty royal family. The mintshipman would pop down to the nearest shop and buy a ton of bacon, loads of eggs, mountains of black pudding and the biggest frying pan on Mintworld. Then he'd chip off some bits of peppermint and make a big fire, onto which he'd put the frying pan and cook everything. He'd serve the mighty breakfast up to the King and his family with a fried slice each and beans for those that wanted them.

After they'd finished their fry-up, the King would wipe his chops and say thank you, but he wanted him to complete another task, which was doing the dishes, even though it wasn't his turn. The mintshipman would grit his teeth and do them anyway. Then the King would say that he quite fancied a cup of tea and oh, the kitchen floor needs cleaning too while you're in there. And the mintshipman would grumble and get on with the job because he really wanted a chance to meet the daughter. Then the dog would run in and mess up the floor again and the mintshipman would say oh for goodness' sake does anybody in this place appreciate anything I do around here? Then the King would say OK, the mintshipman could meet his daughter if he was just going to moan all the time, and he'd give him the key to the tower.

The mintshipman would climb the steps to the top of the tower and unlock the door. He'd be a bit nervous, but still extremely charming and handsome. But then, when he'd walk into the room, he'd see the princess was just a big puppet being operated by the King, who would turn to the mintshipman and say ha ha got you, it's just a joke to get suckers like you to do all the chores, oh, the look on your face and so on. And the mintshipman would say it was a — liberty and not at all funny.

The Pirate Captain angrily flicked Mintworld into his mouth and crunched it up. He was furious at the way these Mintworlders treated each other and decided to be a vengeful god and get rid of the lot of them.

'. . . and that's why there should be legislation to stop buy-to-let landlords taking advantage of easy credit and tax breaks, because it simply prices first-time buyers out of the market,' finished Napoleon.

'Thank you for that,' said the Governor. 'A very illuminating and robust answer. Now, Pirate Captain, you've been uncharacteristically silent for the last hour. Can we have your rebuttal?'

It suddenly dawned on the Pirate Captain that perhaps he wasn't quite as good at concentrating as he thought he was.

He cleared his throat. Then he played for time by tapping his teeth. Then he whistled for a bit. Eventually it was pretty obvious that tapping his teeth and whistling would only cut it for so long, and that he was going to have to actually say something. 'My rebuttal . . . Myyyyy rebuttal.' He paused again and stared at the ceiling. 'Well, you may ask, Governor. Oh yes. And it's quite a rebuttal. It's coming up right about now. Here it comes.'

Everybody looked at him expectantly.

'My rebuttal,' said the Pirate Captain, 'is that Napoleon is so fat, whenever he swims in the sea they put out flood warnings all along the coast.'

The islanders, the Governor, Napoleon and even the pirates gasped.

'It's because of the displacement of water, you see,' the Captain continued. 'Rather like a pirate boat, his grotesque obesity causes . . .'

He trailed off. From the look on everybody's faces it began to occur to him that possibly the word 'rebuttal' didn't mean exactly what he thought it did.

'Pirate Captain!' bellowed Napoleon. 'You go too far!' He stormed forward until they were nose to nose. The little general had turned the colour of an aubergine, and he was shaking from the top of his hat to the tip of his leather boots. For a moment, the Pirate Captain thought he was in real trouble. But Napoleon just pulled off his glove and slapped him in the face with it.

'Oh, that's a relief,' exclaimed the Pirate Captain, letting out a big sigh. 'I thought you were going to do something *terrible*.' Out of the corner of his eye he noticed that the pirate crew had all turned ashen, so much so that he couldn't even tell which one was the albino any more. He waved to show them that there was no harm done. 'Don't worry, lads.' He grinned. 'I'm fine. Barely a scratch. In fact, I've been slapped with much worse things than a glove. Black Bellamy slapped me in the face with a dolphin once. Why are you all looking so distraught?'

'We duel at dawn,' said Napoleon.

'Bother,' said the Pirate Captain.

Fourteen

ANKLE-DEEP
IN SHARKS

'Well, number two, it looks like I've done it again,' said the Pirate Captain, reluctantly hefting himself out of his bath. Bleary-eyed he squinted at the clock above the sink. It was 7.30 a.m., which was a time that he hadn't even realised existed until now. 'No matter how often I mention learning from my mistakes, I always seem to end up slap bang in the middle of another life-or-death situation.'

The pirate with a scarf handed the Pirate Captain his best towel, which had some pictures of lions lazing around and 'I've bathed with the lions at Longleat!' written across the top, and tried to affect a philosophical expression. 'I think the trouble is unfortunately the one thing you *have* learned, Captain, is that you usually manage to get away with it, so there's no real deterrent.'

'It's not really my fault. The problem is that my mouth just comes out with these things. And you can't blame me for what my mouth does, can you? Curse this mouth. Do you think it might be possessed?' The Pirate Captain looked in the mirror and made his mouth into a series of shapes that he thought looked demonic.

'It may be impetuous, sir, but it's also bursting with quiet resolve and kissable softness,' said the pirate with a scarf, as tactful as ever.

'I suppose it *is* one of my best features,' sighed the Pirate Captain. 'Still, if it wasn't for the sensuous curve of my lips I think I'd probably cut my mouth off and have done with it. I reckon I could cope perfectly well without one.'

As the pirate with a scarf brushed the Captain's teeth, they both contemplated what life would be like if the Pirate Captain had no mouth. The pirate with a scarf could certainly see an upside, but on balance he thought that he'd miss hearing the Pirate Captain use his mouth to say things like 'scurvy lubbers' and 'Do we have any Coco Pops?'

'Even so, I'm not *too* worried,' continued the Captain, after he had gargled. 'You know what these generals are like. Stand at the back shouting orders and expect the little man to do all the work for them. Would you mind putting my deodorant on for me, number two? My arms are still quite sleepy.'

He lifted his arms. 'But there's no little man to do the work for him this time, is there? Frankly, I doubt he's ever picked up a sword in his life.'

'All France Champion, 1810, 1811, 1812. European Gold Medal four years running. *What Épée?* Man of the Year, 1814,' said the pirate with a scarf.

The Pirate Captain wilted a bit.

'Red pants or blue pants?' asked the pirate with a scarf.

'Red. Do you think there's some sort of ancient martial art that bee-keepers have passed down from generation to generation? Ideally something that I can learn in about twenty minutes while I get dressed?'

'I'm afraid there's nothing in the *Children's Golden Treasury of Bee Stories* along those lines.' The pirate with a scarf paused. 'I know it's not in your nature, Captain, but it's really not too late to flee. Nobody would think any less of you.'

The Captain snorted imperiously. 'You know me. "Flee" isn't in my vocabulary. By which I don't mean "flee" isn't in my vocabulary in the same way that "rebuttal" isn't in my vocabulary. I know what "flee" means. In fact, I know what both spellings of the word "flee" mean, double "e" and "ea". But my point is this – the Pirate Captain doesn't flee.' He did his resolute face and stared out of the bathroom window. All of a sudden his eyes lit up. 'And he doesn't need to, because he's just come up with a maverick yet brilliant idea that pretty much guarantees him victory. Only I'm not going to say what it is, number two, because I don't want to undermine the impending drama for you.'

There was a real spirit of carnival down on the beach. As ever, the pirate crew demonstrated a touching faith in their Captain which bordered on the delusional, so they were waving banners, blowing horns and joking with the islanders. Enterprising types were selling snacks and football rattles. They all cheered as the Pirate Captain and the pirate with a scarf appeared over the brow of the hill. The Captain was wearing his best blousy shirt, his beard was gleaming in the early morning light and he'd polished all his gold teeth. As he strode manfully towards the shore, the only thing that could have made him look even more heroic than he already did would have been the theme to *Flash Gordon* playing in the background, but it was a hundred and seventy years too early for that.

'So, this is dawn, is it?' the Captain muttered, staring out at the horizon. 'I have to admit, it's very pretty the way it does all those orangey colours. I didn't know sky got up to that kind of thing.' He turned to Jennifer, who was carrying his cutlass. 'Well, Jennifer. Here I am, facing almost certain death. Possibly these are my last few minutes on Earth. You know what might be a nice send-off?'

'Sorry, Pirate Captain,' said Jennifer, giving him a warm but platonic embrace. 'I already told you I won't do that. But good luck anyhow, we're all rooting for you.'

The crowd murmured amongst themselves excitedly as, from the other end of the beach, Napoleon appeared. He marched forward with a businesslike air, kitted out in a set of immaculate white fencing gear. The pirate who followed fashion reckoned Napoleon had already lost the most important battle, mainly because the pirate who followed fashion didn't read many books and thought Napoleon had a sieve on his face. The two men stood toe to toe and everything fell silent, except for the rolling Atlantic Ocean which seemed pretty disinterested in the whole affair and went on crashing against the rocks that lined either side of the bay.

'Ladies and gentlemen,' said the Governor, gravely. 'In all my years on St Helena, never have I had to oversee an event as regrettable as the duel you are about to witness. Please! Don't cheer! It's horrible. I would beseech both parties one last time to resolve this in some more amicable way.'

'Fair enough,' said the Pirate Captain, shrugging. He held a conciliatory hand out to his rival. 'How about a game of Monopoly? I'll let you be the dog, if you like. And to show you just how amicable I'm feeling, I don't even mind if you want me to be the wheelbarrow. Normally I hate being the wheelbarrow.'

'I am sorry,' replied Napoleon, cricking his neck. 'But we Corsicans are a proud breed. Only blood can wipe the stain from my honour.'[27]

'Honestly, Napoleon,' said the Captain with a sigh. 'That doesn't even make sense. How can blood wipe away a stain? It's just going to make an even bigger stain. White wine might do the trick.'

'Gentlemen, please take your positions,' said the Governor, 'which we have marked with little sandcastles – the Pirate Captain's being a tiny ship and Napoleon's a miniature Versailles. Thanks to the St Helena Competitive Sandcastle Group for that.'

A group of islanders cheered.

'They'd like me to remind everyone that they meet every Tuesday morning at nine down here on the beach. Bring your own bucket and spade.'

---

27   The term 'vendetta' comes from Corsica, which had a strict social code whereby any perceived insult would result in death. Between 1683 and 1715 it is estimated that a quarter of the population (30,000 people) were killed as a result. And in 1954 a donkey strayed into a neighbour's garden, leading to a ten-year feud and two deaths.

The Pirate Captain liked sandcastles and made a mental note to pop along next Tuesday, before remembering that there was a distinct possibility he'd be cut to pieces before then.[28]

'Now, I want a good clean fight to the death. No scratching, biting, goading, bombing, petting, or hitting each other with tables, ladders or chairs. Sexy distractions are strictly forbidden.' The Governor looked up at the stormy sky. 'And if you could get it over with before this drizzle turns into proper rain, I'm sure we'd all be very grateful.'

Napoleon swept his rapier from its scabbard. He bowed to the Pirate Captain and raised his blade. '*En garde!*'

'Aaarr. That means put your cutlass up, doesn't it? You know, for this to be fair I really should be going backwards up a staircase.'

The Pirate Captain decided to start the duel the same way he played chess – by closing his eyes and making as much noise as possible.

---

28 Myrtle Beach in South Carolina is the current holder of the World's Tallest Sandcastle record – 49.55 feet.

Cutlass hit rapier and steel rang on steel and there were even some sparks, which delighted everyone because it looked really dramatic. The Captain lunged forward energetically, his beard shook and his earrings jangled. Things seemed to be going so well he even decided to do a little pirouette between blows, as Napoleon edged backwards under the onslaught.

'I'm no expert on fencing,' said the pirate in red, watching from the sidelines, 'but you have to admire Napoleon's parrying. He's not really moving anything but his wrist, is he?'

'I think they're toying with each other, look-ing for weaknesses,' said the pirate in green. 'Napoleon's main weakness seems to be that he looks a little bored, whilst the Pirate Captain's main weakness is that he's already hopelessly out of breath and has no technique whatsoever.'

'Why on earth is he twirling about like that?' asked Jennifer. 'Do you think he's drunk?'

'Don't worry,' said the pirate with a scarf, trying to look as hopeful as possible. 'The Captain told me that he has "something up his sleeve".'

Every time the Pirate Captain swung, he was annoyed to find Napoleon's blade already there. He aimed a blow right at his opponent's neck, but the general simply hopped to one side, and the Pirate Captain's momentum nearly sent him tumbling onto the sand. Napoleon whirled around and sliced dangerously at the Captain's unprotected left side. 'A surprise flank attack,' Napoleon announced with a grin, 'similar to that which secured my victory at Castiglione.'

'You can't compare my belly with a city,' said the Pirate Captain, frantically back-pedalling. 'That's a rubbish metaphor.'

'Simile, Pirate Captain, it's a simile. Now for a sustained assault on your front lines.'

Napoleon lunged at the Pirate Captain's chest. The point of his blade cut through the fabric of the Captain's blousy white shirt but he managed to twist out of harm's way just in time.

'Oh! The big man swerves at the last minute,' said the Pirate Captain, in a commentator voice. 'It's an *incredible recovery* and the crowd go wild!' He made a 'crowd roar' sound with his mouth.

'*Concentrate*!' said Napoleon. 'It's bad enough that you're using illegal fencing manoeuvres, but the commentary is too much. Stand still, damn you!'

'And it's not looking good for the little general, as the Pirate Captain feints to the left, then to the right and – AAAHHH!'

The Pirate Captain's arm was bleeding. He'd hardly even seen Napoleon move. The watching pirates were aghast. For years the Captain had persuaded them that his veins ran with brine, and then recently he'd claimed that actually it was honey. But now they could see it, pouring from his bicep, it looked a lot like normal red blood. They couldn't help but feel a little disappointed.

Staggering backwards, the Captain tried to imagine again what he would do if this was a game of chess. But the analogy didn't stretch that far, because he realised that by this point he would have 'accidentally' knocked the board on the floor with a sweep of his arm and stormed off in a huff.

Napoleon seemed unstoppable. He leaped over a rock and jabbed again with his rapier, and the Pirate Captain let out a tremendous surprised roar as it speared about three inches into his shoulder. He looked down at himself in shock, not sure which was worse: the excruciating pain or the fact that his mermaid tattoo now had a big hole in her forehead, which frankly made her a lot less attractive.

'Strike two!' said Napoleon. 'The crabs shall make a meal of your blood, Pirate Captain. And the seagulls will feast upon your pleasant, open face.'

Another blow from Napoleon sent the Captain's cutlass clattering uselessly away. The situation looked bleak. And though it was a bit earlier in the proceedings than he would have liked, the Pirate Captain decided it was time to unveil his Secret Weapon. He swerved to avoid a swipe that almost chopped his hat in two, and yanked back his right sleeve.

'What's he doing?' said the pirate with a hook for a hand. 'Is he going to use his cartoon octopus tattoo as a distraction?'

'He seems to be wearing a falconry glove,' said the pirate in green, squinting at the spectacle unfolding in front of them. 'And for some reason he's stuck some currants to it.'

'Maybe he's hungry?' said the pirate with long legs.

The Pirate Captain waggled his forearm. 'Go! Fly! Fly, my bees! Attack!'

Three drowsy bees flew off the glove into the air. One circled around the Captain's head and stung him on the ear. The second fell dead to the sand. The third flew at Napoleon, changed its little bee mind and then headed out to sea.[29]

'Oh dear,' said Jennifer. 'That was his secret weapon? *Bees?*'

'Why?! Why have you betrayed me?' bellowed the Pirate Captain, sinking to his knees. 'You bees! How could you do this? Oh cruel, treacherous fate! My bees! My traitor bees!'

The pirate crew knew that their captain had a

---

29 One of the few things people can say that's more annoying than 'we only use 10 per cent of our brains!' is 'According to the laws of physics bees shouldn't be able to fly!' In actual fact, experiments carried out by Michael H. Dickinson at Caltech using high-speed photography and a big robotic wing showed that bees are able to fly basically because they flap their wings really, *really* fast.

'unique world view', but they realised that people who didn't know him very well might just think he was a bit mentally ill. Looking at him now, drenched with rain, blood running down his arm, waving his hands about and shouting to the heavens about being 'King of the Bees', he did look a *little* unhinged. Confronted with this spectacle Napoleon seemed suddenly less confident, almost as if he were a bit embarrassed by the entire situation. The Pirate Captain took advantage of Napoleon's brief hesitation, and he clambered away up one of the craggy rocks that lined the bay.

'Think fast, Pirate Captain,' said the Pirate Captain, as the General began to advance upon him once more.

The Captain thought fast.

First he thought about burgers. He liked burgers, more than hot dogs but not as much as steak. Then he thought about paper and decided that his favourite size was A5, because he could fold it small enough to go in his pocket without creating an unsightly bulge. Finally he thought about his pirate mentor, Calico Jack, and at last it came to him. He recalled a summer evening in a cherry orchard, when the old man had taught him a move that was both exciting and deadly: the Soaring Barnacle.

The Captain leaped from the rock and backed away down the sand so that he had a bit of a run-up. Then he turned to face Napoleon, paused briefly to wink at his public, and sprinted forward. All of a sudden he dropped to his knees and slid along the ground, waving his arms above his head. Just as he came within striking distance, the Pirate Captain remembered that the Soaring Barnacle was actually a dance move.

'Pirates doing unexpected dance moves' was the kind of thing that fencing instructors tended not to mention, so Napoleon found himself caught completely off guard. There was a *whumping* sound as the Pirate Captain crashed right into the general's midriff, knocking him off his feet and his rapier into the sand. The two men rolled down the beach in an ungainly tangle of limbs. They rolled across the shingle, they rolled through both the sandcastles, and soon they were rolling into the sea.

'In my old job as a Victorian lady,' said Jennifer, 'I had to read a lot of romantic novels. They led me to believe that duelling was both a noble pursuit and the height of civilised combat. I certainly don't remember hair-pulling or wedgies being mentioned.'

'Are they fighting or cuddling? I can't tell,' said the pirate in red.

'They're getting terribly far from the shoreline,' said the Governor. 'Do you think I should call them back? Pirate Captain! Napoleon! Please! This has become most unedifying!'

Unfortunately the Pirate Captain and Napoleon were too busy being engulfed by a great crashing wave to hear a word. Then they were too busy getting swept away in the ocean's roaring currents. And before the watching crowd could do anything, all that was left were two pointy black hats bobbing about in the swell.

Fifteen

AN APPOINTMENT
WITH STABBING!

Three miles out to sea, the Pirate Captain and Napoleon eventually began to realise the scale of their predicament.

'This seems to have got somewhat out of hand,' said the Pirate Captain.

'Yes,' said Napoleon, spitting out a starfish and a mouthful of water. 'It has rather.'

The two of them hauled themselves onto a piece of driftwood and didn't say anything for a while whilst they got their breath back. The currents had carried them so far from the shore by now that St Helena was just a speck on the horizon, and the rolling grey Atlantic stretched out seemingly for ever in all directions, like a boring geography lesson.

'I declare this piece of driftwood the sovereign property of Napoleon,' said Napoleon.

'You can't do that, because I already declared it the sovereign property of the Pirate Captain.'

'You did not.'

'I did. But I said it quietly under my breath, so you probably just didn't hear.'

'Fine. You see that line of lichen? Everything to the left of that is mine. Please stay off my property.'

'Happy to.'

The Captain turned his back on the general and thought about his adventure with Darwin. He stared at his reflection in the water and tried with all his remaining strength to evolve gills.

'Why are you pulling such a ridiculous face?' enquired Napoleon.

'I'm trying to mutate into a mer-person. I'd advise you to do the same, because I think we could be out here some time.'

'How long do you think we might survive on a diet of barnacles?' asked Napoleon, after a couple of hours had passed, more to break the silence than anything else.[30]

'Oh well, I believe they're quite nutritious,' said the Captain, trying to sound upbeat.

---

30 It's possible to live without food for several weeks, but without water you'll be dead in three or four days. The longest solo survival at sea is a Chinese man who survived for 133 days adrift on a raft after his ship was torpedoed during the Second World War.

'Though you'll starve to death long before me, because look.' He nodded at his glove. 'I've still got a couple of dead bees stuck to my glove.'

Napoleon sighed. 'It strikes me, Pirate Captain, that all this has become . . . a trifle petty.'

The Pirate Captain looked at the line of lichen, and at the little French flag and pirate flag they had each carved into their respective halves of driftwood, and he couldn't help but feel that Napoleon might have a point. He tugged at his eyebrow for a moment, and then he picked up one of the bees and held it out to his rival.

'Dead bee, Napoleon?'

'Don't mind if I do. Thank you, Captain.'

The two men chewed thoughtfully on their dead bees for a minute or two.

'Listen,' said the Pirate Captain eventually. 'I really am sorry about that weight remark. I got in a bit of a muddle and thought we were trash-talking, like that time during my adventure in Harlem, but that's no excuse.'

'Perhaps you had a point, Captain.' Napoleon picked a bee leg from between his teeth and patted his belly with a rueful air. 'I have been letting myself go of late.'

'Nonsense. I was just perpetuating unrealistic body standards. I should know better.' The Pirate Captain squinted up at the sun, which had come out from behind a bank of clouds and was now starting to beat down on them remorselessly. 'Wish I hadn't lost my tricorne. This dying of exposure business is going to play havoc with my skin-care regime.'

'I wonder who won the election?' said Napoleon.

'Hardly seems to matter now,' said the Pirate Captain.

'No, I suppose not. In fact, I can't really remember why it seemed so important in the first place.'

The Captain scratched his soggy beard thoughtfully. 'Normally, Napoleon, I have to say, I'm not much of a one for emotional journeys. In fact, I'd go so far as to say I pride myself on remaining completely unchanged by my adventures. But this time, during my brief stay on St Helena, I've come to realise two important home truths. First: bees are fickle *@%$#s who'll let you down soon as look at you. But also, and perhaps more importantly, I've learned that just because I'm never going to be Pirate of the Year, that's no reason to stop doing what I love. Self-worth shouldn't come from awards and trinkets and getting the respect of your peers, it should come from within.'

Napoleon frowned. 'Surely by that logic anybody can declare themselves a success no matter how useless and ineffectual they are? You know, like homeopathy.'

'Well, I didn't say it was a completely coherent personal philosophy,' said the Captain, shrugging.

Napoleon jutted out his chin and gripped the Captain's shoulder. 'Really we are much alike, you and I.'

'You mean the hats?'

'No, Pirate Captain, I mean that we have both of us lost our way. I deluded myself that besting you in various pointless endeavours was somehow a good substitute for conquering the entire known world. But it isn't. It's not even close. I'm not quite sure how I got in such a muddle. The fact is, when it comes to the heart of the matter, we've both been running away from ourselves.'

'The last time I did that it turned out to be a papier-mâché version of me that Black Bellamy had built as a prank,' said the Captain, nodding sagely. 'Scared the living daylights out of me.'

'I mean in a slightly more metaphorical sense, Captain.'

'Aarrrr, got you. Ironic for us to have all these epiphanies whilst facing certain death in the middle of the Atlantic.'

'Very.'

'Don't take it the wrong way, Napoleon, but I'm starting to have one of those delusions where I'm seeing your face, but sat atop a gigantic mouth-watering steak instead of a normal body. You have delicious cupcakes for eyes and a strip of bacon for a mouth.'

'I, too, am suffering hallucinations, Pirate Captain. I keep on thinking I can see a ship over there on the horizon.'

'Yes, I'm having that hallucination too. Oh, and now your ears have turned into lamb cutlets.'

Three Months Later

Sixteen

LOST IN THE
SNOWS OF TERROR

The pirate with a scarf stood on St Helena's little beach, skipped a stone into the sea and stared out towards the horizon. Even though the stone bounced six times before it sank beneath the waves, which the pirate with a scarf was pretty sure must be a world record, his heart felt as heavy as a cannonball. He sighed because he knew that the Pirate Captain, had he been there, would have come up with a much better comparison than 'heavy as a cannonball'. He'd have probably known the weight of some sort of dinosaur, or a special cut of meat, and would have used that instead. 'Heavy as half a stegosaurus or two pork bellies', something along those lines.

'He's not coming back, you know,' said Jennifer, appearing at the pirate with a scarf's side and putting a gentle hand on his shoulder. 'The Captain's gone to that great pirate feast in the sea. The one he was always talking about, where the waitresses all wear those off-the-shoulder, medieval-style lacy tops, and they never run out of grog or chops.'

'I guess so,' the pirate with a scarf said sadly. 'I just hope there's somebody there to wipe the meat grease from his beard in the afterlife. You know what a messy eater he is.'

'Come on, we'll be late. They're about to unveil the memorial.'

A solemn crowd waited outside the St Helena Museum of Natural History and Antiquities, which now had the large red curtain from the town hall tacked onto one of its walls. Everybody looked sad but slim, because they were wearing black, which is flattering to the fuller figure. Several of the gamine lady islanders blew their noses noisily into their handkerchiefs. Even the 'Monstrous Manatee' had come out to pay his respects.

'We're gathered here today to remember our island's two greatest residents,' said the Governor, standing on top of a small box in front of the curtain. 'Now, unfortunately we can't carry out the Pirate Captain's exact wishes for his memorial, because we don't have either the troupe of dancing girls or the swimming pool full of jelly. Nor can we implement Monsieur Bonaparte's desires to the letter, because the technology has yet to be invented that can rearrange the stars in the night sky so that they form a big dot-to-dot picture of his face. But hopefully, were they able to be here today, they would both approve of this little memorial. May it be a lesson to us all.'

He yanked on a piece of rope and the curtain fell away to reveal a large mural. It showed the Pirate Captain and Napoleon, each atop a brightly coloured pony, galloping down a road made out of rainbows whilst an assortment of woodland creatures looked on. At the bottom were the words:

In loving memory of the pirate
captain and napoleon
bonaparte, washed out to sea
whilst having a duel. Why can't
we all just get along?

'Would you like to add a few words, pirate with a scarf?' asked the Governor.

The pirate with a scarf stepped forward and awkwardly traced a little picture in the sand with the toe of his boot. 'I don't really know what to say. It's true the Pirate Captain wasn't perfect. He could be pretty forgetful to be honest. He got through astrolabes like you wouldn't believe. He tended to rely on "running people through" as a substitute for reasoned arguments. And he certainly had some strange ideas about where babies come from. But despite all that—'

The pirate with a scarf stopped dead. Most of the audience grumblingly muttered that they thought this was a pretty poor eulogy, but then they followed the pirate with a scarf's startled gaze and saw two shambling figures emerge from the sea and wander up the beach towards them.

'Sea Monsters!' exclaimed the albino pirate.

'Come to feast on our guts!' wailed the Governor. 'Or whatever bit of anatomy it is sea monsters eat at this time of day.'

As the two figures got closer the pirates saw that it wasn't sea monsters. In fact, it seemed to be a pair of surprisingly burly, bearded washerwomen. They were laughing and having quite an animated chat.

'Hello, you scurvy knaves,' roared one of the washerwomen, in a familiar booming voice. 'What on earth is all this? Where are my dancing girls in jelly?'

'Pirate Captain!' exclaimed the pirates, because that's who it was. They rushed forward, and then checked themselves when, as one, they all had the same thought.

'Are you a ghost or are you a zombie?' asked the albino pirate tentatively. 'If you're a zombie then don't just say "ghost" in order to gain ready access to our brains.'

The Captain patted him on the head reassuringly and looked the mural up and down. 'Not sure you've done justice to my famous hourglass figure,' he sniffed, hands on hips. 'But I like the ponies, they're a nice touch.'

'Your pony is called Starchaser. And Mister Napoleon's is called Moonjumper,' said the pirate in green eagerly. 'I've written some stories about the adventures you get up to riding about on them in the afterlife.'

'And they've done you very well, Napoleon,' added the Captain, turning to the other washerwoman, who the pirates now saw was actually the moonfaced little general. 'Really caught the quiet strength of your eyebrows.'

'Hang on,' said Jennifer. 'Do you mean to say you two like each other now?'

'Yes, it's amazing what five days sharing the same bit of driftwood will do for a relationship,' said Napoleon, winking. 'It's real kill-or-cure stuff. I think they should recommend it to married couples going through difficulties.'

'But where have you *been* all this time? And why *aren't* you in the afterlife?' asked the pirate with gout.

'Like Napoleon says, we drifted around for a while. Endless lapping waves, unremitting tedium, all the usual lost-at-sea stuff. But Neptune must have been in one of his better moods, because just before we got to drawing lots for who got to eat my succulent thighs first, we were picked up by a passing ship. Of course, slightly less fortunately it turned out to be a slave-ship run by those black-hearted brigands from the East India Company. So before you could say "I like ham" we were thrown in the hold and clapped in irons.'

'Dear me. How on earth did you escape?' asked the Governor.

'Aarrr, well. It's a bit of a long story.' The Pirate Captain sat down on a rock, adjusted his frock and lit a cigarette. 'There we were, halfway to the other side of the world, hanging upside down in the bowels of this devil ship, facing certain death or worse . . .'

'. . . and that's how we defeated the combined forces of the East India Company, the Jade Emperor's golden hordes, the King of the Cowboys and the International Crime Cartel, armed only with a piece of seaweed and six barnacles.'

All the pirates and islanders clapped, because it was easily the most exciting tale any of them had ever heard, or would ever be likely to hear, with inciting incidents and second-act climaxes

243

and setbacks and moments of despair and character arcs and long dark nights of the soul and last-minute reprieves in all the right places.

'The only thing I don't quite understand,' said the Governor, frowning, 'is how you ended up emerging from the sea dressed as washerwomen?'

'Oh, let's not get into that right now,' said the Pirate Captain, yawning. 'Because it's a whole other kettle of fish that I may or may not choose to explain at a later date, depending on how the mood takes me.'

'Fair enough, Captain,' said Jennifer. 'We're just happy you're back. Anyhow, you'll be delighted to know that we kept up with the beekeeping. We've become quite proficient at it. It turns out the albino pirate is a bit of a natural.'

'Yes, Captain,' added the Governor happily. 'Famous Nautical Honey is now St Helena's most popular export.'[31]

---

31 In the UK alone it is estimated that bees' contribution to the agricultural economy stands at £1 billion, but this is threatened by the alarming recent spread of Colony Collapse Disorder, which has already wiped out a quarter of America's 2.5 million honeybee colonies.

'Aaarrr, about that,' the Pirate Captain said, absently twirling a lock of beard hair around his finger. 'I hate to disappoint you, lads, but I've had another one of my unpredictable changes of heart.'

'You mean we're going to be pirates again?' asked Jennifer, clapping her hands in delight.

The Captain grinned. 'Maybe I am a bit of an antique when it comes to modern piracy. And possibly we're not the most successful bunch of brigands ever to sail the seven seas. But I still have a glossier beard and better tattoos than any of these young idiots with all their fancy side partings and qualifications. So just as soon as we've patched up the boat, who's up for finding some treasure? Even if it *is* guarded by Giant Crabs with terrible clacking pincers?'

The pirates waved goodbye to Napoleon and the Governor as the pirate boat sailed away from the island. They rubbed their faces against the rigging and happily inhaled the smell of tar and weevils. A few of them fell over, because they'd been on land so long that they hadn't found their sea legs yet, except for the pirate with a hook for a hand, who'd found his sea legs because they were prosthetic and made out of wood, and he kept them safely in a trunk next to his hammock.

'It's good that Mister Napoleon has decided to go back to trying to conquer the world, once he's finished his memoirs,' said the pirate in green.

'And we're glad you decided bee-keeping wasn't being true to yourself, Captain,' said the pirate with a scarf. 'In fact, the lads clubbed together and made you something.'

The pirate with a scarf beckoned to the albino pirate, who stepped forward sheepishly. He handed the Captain a little trophy that appeared to be made mostly from foil and sticky tape. The Pirate Captain held it up in the sunlight and peered at the inscription.

'*For the Pirate Captain*,' he read. '*You'll always be OUR Pirate of the Year. Love, the crew.*' The Captain paused, and bit his lip. 'Boys, I don't know what to say. I mean, obviously this trophy is extremely poorly made and of no monetary value at all, and I don't suppose the judging process was particularly rigorous, but still, I'm touched. Anyhow, it's been a long day and I need to get out of these washerwoman clothes,' said the Pirate Captain, handing the wheel over to his second-in-command and heading towards his cabin.

'Oh, and lads?' The Pirate Captain stopped mid-stride, turned round and pulled a serious face. 'The best thing about the seaside is the Punch and Judy shows.' Then he marched through the big oak doors to his office.

'He's right,' said the pirate in green. 'It *is* the Punch and Judy shows.'

'Especially the bit with the crocodile and the sausages,' said the albino pirate.

And with that, the pirates went downstairs to do some shantying.

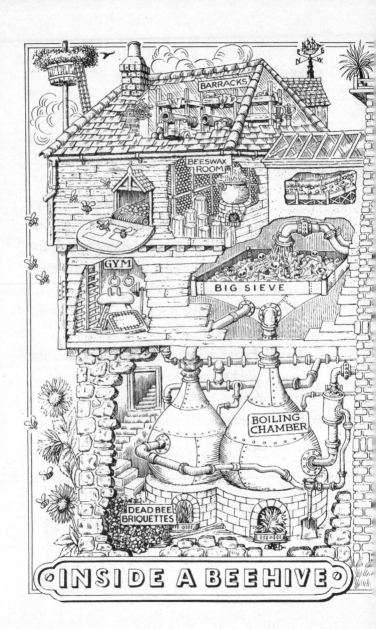

BARRACKS

BEESWAX ROOM

GYM

BIG SIEVE

BOILING CHAMBER

DEAD BEE BRIQUETTES

INSIDE A BEEHIVE

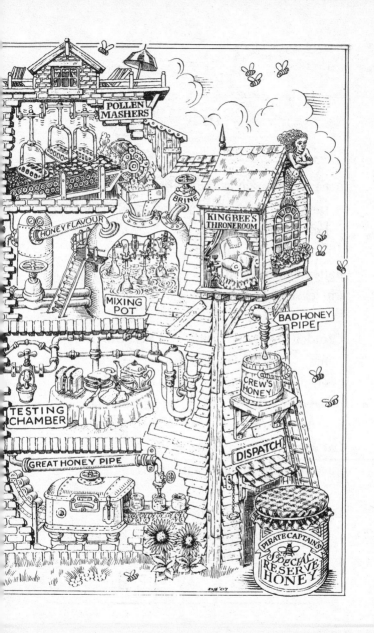

Index

Eagles, pirates admire, 340–780; pirates attempt to live like, 781; egg catastrophe, 783

Flax, 72–76

Giant butterflies, PC replaces crew with, 78–79; PC struggles to make conversation with, 89; get dust everywhere, 130; PC has enough and swats with oar, 131

Girls, remain resolutely unimpressed by pirate books, 1–944

Ham, glazed, 234, 289, 903–1045
Ham, honey-roasted, 678
Ham, Serrano, 29–563
Ham, spiced, 42, 53–59, 89–105, 345
Ham, Tesco Value, 90, 450–503, 834
Ham, tinned, PC calls 'unnatural', 193
Ham, wafer-thin, 12, 24, 42, 98, 134–140
Highlighter pens, PC's collection, 178–234; search for sixth colour, 293

India, PC thinks is 'part of Wales', 99

Tap dancing,90

Ukulele, PC mistakes for guitar and assumes
  he has grown giant-sized, 155
Underwear, PC hangs around kitchen in, 234

Vermin, 903
Voodoo ladies, island of the, 360–362

Women, island of the, 87–89

Yak, 8

Zanzibar, PC sets up badge shop in, 740

Starchaser and Moonjumper

Will return in

Ponies Galore!

Book 9 of the Pony! Adventure Series

Ring 10/11/2020

THE PIRATES! IN AN ADVENTURE WITH SCIENTISTS

St. Julians

14.10.22

NOW A MAJOR MOTION PICTURE

It is 1837, and for the luxuriantly bearded Pirate Captain and his rag-tag pirate crew, life on the high seas has gotten a little dull. With nothing to do but twiddle their hooks and lounge aimlessly on tropical beaches, the Captain decides it's time they had an adventure.

A surprisingly successful boat raid leads them to the young Charles Darwin, in desperate need of their help. And so the pirates set forth for London in a bid to save the scientist from the evil machinations of a diabolical Bishop. There they encounter grisly murder, vanishing ladies, the Elephant Man – and have an exciting trip to the zoo.

*

'Gideon Defoe definitively puts the "Ho ho!" –
and, indeed, the "Yo!" – into pirating'
CAITLIN MORAN

*

'Very funny, very silly and highly original'
ESQUIRE

*

'This book has cult smash tattooed all over it'
THE LIST

ORDER YOUR COPY:
BY PHONE: +44 (0)1256 302 699; **BY EMAIL:** DIRECT@MACMILLAN.CO.UK
DELIVERY IS USUALLY 3–5 WORKING DAYS.
FREE POSTAGE AND PACKAGING FOR ORDERS OVER £20.

ONLINE: WWW.BLOOMSBURY.COM/BOOKSHOP
PRICES AND AVAILABILITY SUBJECT TO CHANGE WITHOUT NOTICE.

WWW.BLOOMSBURY.COM

B L O O M S B U R Y